I0587597

William Sharp

# The Laughter of Peterkin

A Retelling of Old Tales of the Celtic Wonderworld

William Sharp

**The Laughter of Peterkin**
*A Retelling of Old Tales of the Celtic Wonderworld*

ISBN/EAN: 9783744712132

Printed in Europe, USA, Canada, Australia, Japan

Cover: Foto ©Andreas Hilbeck / pixelio.de

More available books at **www.hansebooks.com**

# THE LAUGHTER OF PETERKIN.

"A RETELLING OF OLD TALES OF THE CELTIC WONDERWORLD." by

## · FIONA MACLEOD ·

DRAWINGS · BY · SUNDERLAND · ROLLINSON ·

TO

ISLA,

EILIDH,

FIONA,

AND

IVOR

# CONTENTS



4

# ILLUSTRATIONS

## By SUNDERLAND ROLLINSON

# The Laughter of Peterkin

# The Laughter of Peterkin

A T the rising of the moon, Peterkin awoke,
and laughed.  He was in his little white
bed near the open window, so that when a
moonbeam wavered from amid the branches
of the great poplar, falling suddenly upon his
tangled curls and yellowing them with a ripple
of pale gold, it was as though a living thing
stole in out of the June night.

He had not awaked at first.  The moon-
beam seemed caught in a tangle: then it
glanced along a crescent tress on the pillow:
sprang back like a startled bird: flickered
hither and thither above the little sleeping
face: and at last played idly on the closed
eyelids with their long dark eyelashes.  It was
then that Peterkin awoke.

When he opened his eyes he sat up, and
so the moonbeam fell into the two white cups

of his tiny hands. He held it, but like a yellow eel it wriggled away, and danced mockingly upon the counterpane.

With a sleepy smile he turned and looked out of the window. How dark it was out there! That white moth which wavered to and fro made the twilight like a shadowy wall. Then upon this wall Peterkin saw a great fantastic shape. It grew and grew, and spread out huge arms and innumerable little hands: and in its shadow-face it had seven shining eyes. Peterkin stared, awe-struck. Then there was a dance of moonshine, a cascade of trickling, rippling yellow, and he saw that the shape in the night was the familiar poplar, and that its arms were the big boughs and branches where the spotted mavis and the black merle sang each morning, and that the innumerable little hands were the ever-tremulous, ever-dancing, round little leaves, and that the seven glittering eyes were only seven stars that had caught among the topmost twigs.

## II

Peterkin was very sleepy, but before his head sank back to the pillow he saw something which caused him to hold his breath, and made his eyes grow so round and large that they were like the little pools one sees on the hillside.

Every here and there he saw tiny yellow and green lives slipping and sliding along and in and out of the branches of the poplar. Sometimes they were all pale yellow, like gold ; sometimes of a shimmering green ; sometimes so dusky that only by their shining eyes were they visible. At first he could not clearly distinguish these unfamiliar denizens of the great poplar. The vast green pyramid seemed innumerously alive. Then gradually he saw that each delicate shape was like a human being : little men and women, but smaller than the smallest children, smaller even than dolls. They were all laughing and chasing each other to and fro. Some slid swiftly down an outspread branch, and then dropped on to a green leafy billow or plunged into an inscrutable maze : others swung by the little crook at the end of each leaf, and laughed as they were blown this way and that by puffs of air : and a few daring ones climbed to the topmost sprays of the topmost boughs and held up tiny white hands like daisies. These wished to clasp the moonshine. As well might a fish try to catch the moon-dazzle on the water! No wonder Peterkin laughed.

Ever and again a delicate sweet singing came from the moonshine-folk. Peterkin listened, but could hear no words he knew. Perhaps there were no words at all, or mayhap he himself knew too few. But the singing was strangely familiar. Sometimes when mother sang, surely he had heard it: as far back, farther back, than memory could take him, he had heard some echo of it. Cradle-sweet it was, that dim snatch of a fugitive strain. And, too, had he not heard something of it in the wind, when that went whispering through the grass and in and out of the wild-rose thicket, or when it lifted and waved a great wing and fanned the trees into vast swaying flames of green? Yes, even in the fire he had heard it. When the orange and red flames flickered among the coals, or caught the sap in the pine-logs and grew into yellow and blue with hearts of purple, he had heard a faint far-off music.

Peterkin gave a little gasp when a sudden wave of shadow, trailed across the poplar by a long slow-travelling cloud, swept from bough to bough.  It was as though all the singing, laughing, dancing folk had been drowned.

He stared through the darkness, but there was nothing to be seen.  He shivered.  It was lonely out there.  Again he heard a sound as of a remote singing.  As before, he could not hear what the words were.  But, once more, it was not all unfamiliar.  It was sadder than anything that dimly he remembered, save the long mournful crooning of a Gaelic cradle-song, sadder than any flame-whisper in a waning fire, or than any cadence of the wind in the grass, or among the thickets of wild rose.


## III


Next night Peterkin lay awake a long time, hoping to see the moonshine-folk again.  He had spoken of them, but was told that there were no little people in the poplar.  At first this was the more strange to him, for had he not seen them?  Then, after he had scrupulously examined the branches from beneath as well as at a distance, he comforted himself with the thought that, while there might be no little people actually living in the poplar, they came into the tree on the flood of the moonshine.

But that night there was no moon-flood. A south wind had arisen at sundown, and had shepherded from beyond the hills a medley of strayed clouds : these, intricately interwoven, now spread from horizon to horizon, obliterating the stars and obscuring even the radiance of the new-risen moon.

If there were no moonlight, and therefore no little yellow and green lives with bright shining eyes, there was a strange exquisite whispering that grew into music sweeter than any which Peterkin had ever heard.

He rose and crept stealthily from his bed to the door. It was ajar, and he looked, half-fearfully, half-wonderingly, into the open passage. How long and dark it was, and haunted by unfamiliar shadows : but, clasping the skirts of his nightgown close to him, he ran swiftly to the balustrade at the far end.

There the stair lamp shed a comfortable glow. Peterkin looked warily down the stairs, into the hall, along the closed or opened rooms. There was no one stirring. The front door too was open, for the night was warm, or perhaps some one had strayed without.

The child stood awhile, hesitating. Then he slipped down the stairway like a swift moon-beam. For the first time he realized he was only a little child, when he passed the great antlered stag's-head in the hall, and the high stand hung with coats and hats, the raiment of giants as they seemed, and mysteriously life-like.

But once in the open air he lost all fear. True, a great mass of rhododendrons ran close to the avenue to the right, and through this the path meandered to the gardens behind the house: but there was nothing unfamiliar about their gloom, for Peterkin loved their green shadowy depths at noon, and their frag-rant dusk when the long shadows on the lawn slept longer and bluer, till they sank invisibly into the grass.

Old Donal McDonal the gardener, on his way through the shrubberies, rubbed his eyes: for he thought he saw a sprite. He could have sworn, he said to Mairgred Cameron the cook, after he entered the house, that he had seen a small white ghost flitting from bush to bush. Both shook their heads, and wondered if the White Lady were come again, that apparition which legend averred was to be seen by mortal eyes once in every generation, and always before some tragic event or death itself.

But as for Peterkin he had no thought of such things. He was now in the garden, eager in his quest of the little people who hide among leaves and grass, and love the dusk and the moonlit dark.

He had no fear as he ran to and fro along the grassy ways. Why should he be afraid of the dark? There was nothing there to frighten him, or any child.

For a time he ran to and fro, or crept warily among the lilac bushes. His little white figure drifted hither and thither like a moth. Once he was still, when he stood, shimmering white, among the lilies of the valley, which clustered among their green sheaths at the far end of the garden. Here, a few days ago, he had buried a dead bird he had found under a net. It was a thrush, the gardener had told him, puzzled at the slow tears which welled from the eyes of the little lad. And now Peterkin wondered if the bird were awake.

He had gone to Ian Mor, who was staying with his father and mother, and told him about the buried bird: and Ian had comforted him with this tale :—

"Long ago there was a great king. He had the wisdom of wisdom, as the saying is. One day the plague came to his kingdom, and he lost the three lives which were dearest to him in all the world. These were his mother, his wife, and his little son.

"This king was a poet and dreamer, as well as a great warrior and prince, and he had ever been wont to have communion with the powers and sweet influences which are behind the innumerable veils of the world. Through these he had come to know the mystery of the Spirit of Life.

"With this Eternal Spirit he held communion in his deep sorrow. It was then that he learned how what is beautiful cannot pass, for beauty is like life that is mortal, but whose essence does not perish. In fragrance, in colour, in sweet sound, somehow and somewhere, that which is beautiful is transmuted when suddenly changed or slain.

"So he prayed to the Spirit of Life that his dear ones might not pass from him utterly.

"On the morrow, when he rose and went into his favourite place in the royal gardens, a secret hollow in a glade of ilex and pine, he saw a fountain of exceeding beauty. The spray rose dazzling white against the sombre green of the old trees, and seemed to be alive with a myriad rainbow-spirits, who ceaselessly flashed their wings as they darted hither and thither. The king was looking upon this, entranced by its sunny loveliness, when he noticed a white dove flying round the high sunlit fount, and at the hither margin of the water a cream-white dappled fawn, which stooped its graceful neck and drank.

"The king marvelled; for not only had there never been any fountain in that place, but he knew that no wild fawn could wander there from the distant forests, and no dove had he ever seen so snowy white and with wings radiant as though stained by the rainbow-hues of the flying spray.

"Suddenly it was as though a mist fell from his eyes. He saw and understood. His old mother, his wife, his little son, had not passed away, although they were dead. His mother had been fair and beautiful even in her white-hair years; and of the beauty of his wife, whom he loved so passing well, the poets had sung from one end of the land to another; while his little son had been held to be so perfect that there was none like him.

"And now the king saw that the beauty of his mother had passed into a living fount of waters, whose spray cooled the air and made a sound of aerial music and a laughing radiance everywhere ; and that the beauty of the woman whom he had loved so passing well was transmuted into the wild fawn which drank at the water's edge ; and that the beauty of his little son was now the white dove which beat its wings in the rainbow spray.

" The king rejoiced therein with a great joy. Many of his people thought him mad, but he smiled at that saying, and with grave eyes prayed that that madness would come to all true and noble souls in his kingdom.

" For a year and a day this joy was his. Then the fountain ceased to rise, and the dove to beat its pinions in the spray, and the wild fawn to drink at the water's edge. The rumour went from mouth to mouth that this was because the plague had come again. The king was heavy with sorrow, for he had taken his deepest happiness in the beauty of these three lovely things, as, of yore, in the beauty of his aged mother, and in the beauty of the woman whom he loved, and in the beauty of his little son. So once again he remembered how he had been helped.  With shame at his heart he upbraided himself because he had lived too much to the things of the moment and so had lost touch with those which were of the enduring life.  That night he spent in unspoken prayer and prolonged meditation ; and at dawn on the morrow he went slowly and sadly forth, hoping against hope that his life might be gladdened again.

" The sun rose as he crossed the glade of ilex and pine.  There was no fountain, as he well knew ; but where the fountain had been he saw a garth of wild hyacinths, of a blue so wonderful that no Maytide sky was ever more delicately wrought of azure and purple.  And above this were two little brown birds, which sang with so sweet voice and bewildered rapture that his heart melted within him.

" Then he knew that in these new joys he had found again the beauty he had lost.

" When, in the change of the days, the hyacinths spilt their blue wave into the rising green of the fern, and the birds ceased singing their lovely aerial songs, the king no longer grieved, for now he knew that what was beautiful would not perish but drift from change to change.

"And so it was. For when, weary of his pain, he went forth one night to the lovely glade of ilex and pine, he saw the ground white with the little blooms we call Stars of Bethlehem, and among these a glow-worm lay and glowed like a lamp in a white wilderness, and from an ancient ilex came the voice of a nightingale.

" Thus the king was comforted.

" And so you too, Peterkin," added Ian Mor, "need not sorrow too much for your little dead bird. It will live again mayhap in the fragrance of a lily or in the beauty of a rose. It will rise again, Peterkin."

This tale had sunk deeply into the child's mind, and perhaps all the more so because the words, and the meaning behind the words, were sometimes beyond him. But he understood well the drift of what Ian Mor had told him.

He was prepared for any miracle. If his little bird should rise through the brown earth and ascend singing towards the stars ; or if he should hear a song and see no bird ; or if a fount should well from where its body lay ; or if a rare bloom should spring from the earth ; or if a fragrance, new and sweet, should reach him—if one of these things should happen, or anything akin, it would be no surprise to him.

But while he was still wondering, he heard voices.

"Peterkin!  Peterkin!"

He did not answer, but laughing low to himself, crept in among the lilies-of-the-valley, and lay there, himself like a white bloom.  The voices came near, nearer, and passed by. Peterkin's heart smote him, for he heard the pain in the calling voices; but it was so cool and quiet there among the lilies, and it was so sweet to be out of sight of every one and lost, that he could not break the spell.

What if he were to be found by the elfin-folk and led into fairyland?  He thrilled both with fear and eager delight at the thought.  Surely even now he heard the delicate music of the lily-bells?

Peterkin did not know that he had a neighbour.  Suddenly, he heard a faint rustle.  Ah, it was one of the Shee—one of the little people!  Mayhap it was the green Harper, of whom Ian Mor had told him, or one of the seven star-crowned queens, or the haughty Midir, with a peacock's feather in his moon-gold hair, or Fand, who walked in fairy dew, or—or——

And then Peterkin saw who his neighbour was. From under a stone, beset by lily-sheaths, a small toad crawled. Its strange bright eyes were fixed upon the staring child, whom, however, it did not seem to heed after it had once examined this strange white creature who lay among the lilies.

Suddenly Peterkin began to laugh. The toad sat still, solemnly regarding him. Peterkin laughed the more. Once the toad gave a short jump, though this was not from fear, or even from lack of interest in his unfamiliar neighbour, but because a gnat had come temptingly almost within reach of his long, thin, serpentine tongue.

" Tell me, toad," Peterkin said at last, "why are you so funny ?"

Whether it was because the toad was not given to gaiety, or whether his disappointment about the gnat had soured him, he did not respond save by an unwinking stare. After a while it shot out its tongue, as though it were speculating as to Peterkin's flavour as a pleasant morsel, or perhaps only to find if he were within reach.

This was too much for Peterkin, who rolled back among the lilies, crushing the little white bells into a floating fragrance. But, alas, that betraying laughter!

Peterkin was still in its throes when he heard a voice falling upon him as though out of the skies.

"Ah, there you are, you little rascal! How you frightened us all, and what a hunt we have had!"

Almost before he recognised the voice of Ian Mor, Peterkin was seized and lifted high into the air.

"Don't be angry, Ian," the child whispered. "I came out to see the fairies. And then I ran on here to see if the little dead bird had come out of the earth again."

"And have you seen a fairy, Peterkin?"

"I don't know. I saw a toad."

"What did the toad do?"

"It looked at me till I laughed. Then it put out its tongue, and I laughed and laughed and laughed."

"I'm thinking that toad must have been a fairy in disguise, Peterkin. But now come: I am going to carry you back to your bed."

And whether it was because of Peterkin's

escape into the garden, or what vaguely came to him there, or what Ian Mor told him as he carried him homeward in his arms, he did hear the horns of elf-land that night, and did see the gathering of the Shee in the moonshine. But it was in a drowsy hollow in the dim wood of sleep, wherein the birds were white soft-pinioned dreams, and the moon waxed and waned like the lily that sinks and rises in dark pools.

## IV

In those first fragments of Peterkin's experiences, all his life was foreshadowed. Wonder, delight, longing, laughter—the four winds of childhood—these blew for him through his first few years, through childhood and boyhood and youth. He is a man now; but though the laughter is rarer and the longing deeper and more constant, there still blow through the dark glens and wide sunlit moors of his mind the four winds of Laughter, Longing, Wonder, and Delight.

As year after year went by, his mind became a storehouse of all that was most beautiful and marvellous in the Celtic wonder-world. It is no wonder this, since he had for story-teller Ian Mor, and Eilidh whom Ian loved; and knew every shepherd on the hillsides of Strachurmore, and every fisherman on the shores of Loch Fyne. The old ballads, the old romances, the strange fragments of the Ossianic tales, the lore of fairydom, fantastic folk-lore, craft of the woodlands, all of the outer and inner life grew into and became interwrought with the fibre of his most intimate being.

I am not here telling the story of Peterkin himself. He stands, indeed, for many children rather than for one, for many lives and not an individual merely.

In a sense, therefore, Peterkin is not merely a little child, a boy, a youth, who went through his years gladly laughing, mysteriously wondering, wrought to pain and joy, to suffering and delight, by all he saw and heard and inwardly learned; but a type of the Wonder-Child, and so a brother to all children, to poets, and dreamers.

Of the many tales of old times which Peterkin loved, none did he dwell upon with so much delight as those three which are familiar throughout Ireland and Gaelic Scotland as

"The Three Sorrows of Story-Telling." In " The Children of Lir," in " Deirdre and the Sons of Usna," in " The Children of Turenn," he found pre-eminently the haunting charm and sad exquisite beauty which are the colour and fragrance of the Celtic genius. And though in his manhood he turned with deeper emotion to tales such as " Dermid and Grainne," or " The Amadan Mor," it was of these early favourites that he loved to think, that he loved to re-read, to hear again, to re-tell.

That is why, therefore, I have chosen to make this book essentially a re-telling of the beautiful old tales of " The Three Sorrows," so familiar once to our Gaelic ancestors, and still, in however crude a form, the most popular of all the tales of the Gael. They are sad, it is true, because all the old beautiful tales are sad ; but it is a sadness which is a fragrance about an exquisite bloom, and that bloom wrought of joy and keen delight. They were not sad, they who lived the old, joyous, heroic life ; in some poignant vicissitude, some sudden slaying, some passing of a bright flame into a melancholy wane, we see a sad gleam about the end of their days, and, seeing thus the fortuitous coming and going of life and death, read into the old chronicles a melancholy which often is not there.

Of course, a tale such as " The Fate of the Children of Lir "—probably the story known above all others among the children of Western Scotland and Ireland—is sad with another sadness, that of prolonged and unmerited suffering.  But to the Gaelic mind, at least, this is redeemed by the sense of heroic endurance, of the deep unselfish devotion of a lovely womanly type such as is represented by Fionula, and perhaps, above all, by the music and beauty which were the sweet doom of Fionula and her brothers.

But to me not one of them is sad, save with beauty.  For through all I hear the sound of Peterkin's laughter.  Sometimes it was aroused by an episode ; sometimes it leapt like a hound along the trail of vagrant thoughts ; sometimes it came and went as an eddying wind, none knowing whence or whither.

This laughter of Peterkin has become for me one of the sweet wonderful voices of nature— the four winds of Childhood : Wonder, Delight, Longing, and Laughter.  Ah, children, children, to one and all I wish the golden fortune of Peterkin.

## V

When Peterkin was still a child he was familiar with tales of the old world which now-a-days we keep from children, because they are not old enough to understand. That, I fear, is more because we ourselves do not understand, or are out of sympathy. Is a child more likely to be hurt, or to be nobly attuned to the chant-royal of life, by acquaintance with stories of vivid and beautiful human love such as that of Nathos and Darthool, or Dermid and Grainne? Surely, what is beautiful is not a thing to be feared; and though, alas! so many of us do now indeed dread beauty and feel toward it a strange baffled aversion, there are others who know it to be the profoundest and most exquisite mystery in life.

To Peterkin at any rate there was never anything but what was stirring and heroic and full of charm and beauty in these old tales: and through all his days their atmosphere was in his mind, so that he made life fairer for himself and others.

Few stories delighted him more than the wild folk-lore tales which he heard from the shepherds and fishermen, or than those which he was told on Iona. It was to that island he

was taken when he was still a child, at a time
when the shadow of death darkened his young
life.   But there, staying with Ian Mor and with
Eilidh, his wife, he lived the happiest months of
his early years, and came closer to the beauty
of the past and to the beauty of the present
than ever before or after.

It was on Iona that he first heard the
"Three Sorrows of Story-Telling," though
that of Nathos and Darthool—or of "The
Sons of Usna," as it is generally called—was
rather overheard by him as Ian related it to
Eilidh, than told to him direct.

Throughout the first months of his stay in
Iona, Peterkin was told something daily by
Ian Mor, so that, child as he was, he became
familiar with strange names and peoples of the
past, as well as with all the wonders of the
living world.   True, there was thus in his
mind a jumble of the past and the present, and
Columba was more real to him than McCailin
Mor himself, and Finn and Cuchulain, Ossian
and Oscar and Dermid as vivid and actual as
any fisherman of Iona.

When he was old enough to follow aright,
Ian Mor told him, anew and in his own way,
the three famous tales which follow.

# The Tale of the Four
# White Swans

"The cold and cruel fate that overtook
    The children of the great De Danann, Lir,
    Is of the Sorrow-stories of our isle.
    This sorrow-tale indeed is old and young ;
    Old, for so many hundred years have gone
    Since last beneath the midnight shimmering star
    Was heard the music of the birds of snow :
    Young, for amid the bright-eyed tuneful Gael
    The sorrows of the snowy-breasted four
    Are told again to-day, and shall be told
    Long as the children of Milesius last
    To people Banba's hills and pleasant vales."

*The Three Sorrows of Story-Telling :*
"The Children of Lir,"
*trs. by Dr. Douglas Hyde.*

As she touched Fionula, Lir's fair young daughter became a
beautiful snow-white swan.

*To face p.* 33.]

# The Tale of the Four White Swans

THE story that I will tell you now is one of the most famous among all the peoples of the Gael. It is called sometimes " The Tale of the Four White Swans," sometimes " The Fate of the Children of Lir," sometimes simply " Fionula,"[1] because of the beauty and tenderness of Lir's daughter.

The tale is of the old far-off days. It was old when Ossian was a youth, and Fionn heard it as a child from the lips of grey-beards. Often I have spoken to you, Peterkin, of the Danann folk, the Tuatha-De-Danann who lived in the lands of our race before the foreign peoples came and drove the ancient dwellers in

[1] In Gaelic, the name of Lir's daughter is *Fionnghuala*, and is variously given in English as Fionula, Fionnuola, Finoola, and Finola.

Ireland and Scotland to the hills and remote places. When men allude to them now in this late day, they speak of the Dedannans (as they are often called) as the Hidden Folk, the Quiet People, the Hill Folk, and even as the Fairies. It is natural, therefore, that years are as dust in the chronicles of this lost race. They live for hundreds of years where we live for ten; and so it is that the foam of time is white against the brief wave of our life, when against the mighty and long reach of theirs it is but flying spray.

You have heard Eilidh singing the song of the Four White Swans. It is a music that hundreds of tired ears have heard. It is so sweet, Peterkin, that old men grow young, and old women are girls again, and weary hearts ache no more, and dreams and hopes become real, and peace puts out her white healing hand.

" Have you heard that singing, Ian ? "

"Yes, my boykin, often. And you, too, shall often hear it. It is in lonely places, in lonely hours, that you shall hear it. It is a beautiful strange sound, and so old and so wonderful that in it you will hear the beating of the heart of the world thousands of years ago.

But first I will tell you the story of the Four Swans, and then we can speak again of the strange singing I have heard at times, and that you often shall hear."

The Dedannans were the most wonderful and happy people in the world till they became discontented with what the unknown and beautiful gods had given them. Then they split into sections, and some sought one vain thing and some another, and in the end all found weariness. Their wise men knew that as long as they were at one no enemy could prevail against them; but it has never been the way of the unquiet to believe in the old wisdom, and so feuds arose, and the Fairy Host itself—as the great array of the warriors of the Tuatha-De-Danann was called—ceased to be invincible, because the banners blew to the four winds.

Not all their ancestral sojournings in the dim lands of the East, nor in the ages of their migration to the country of fjords which has its whole length in the sea, nor in Alba, that is now Scotland, nor Eiré, that is now Ireland, not all they had learned in their remote past helped them against the undoing of their own folly.

It has been said that the Dedannans never fought against men till the Milesians, the warriors of Miled out of some land in the south—the land, mayhap, we know as Spain—came against them upon the banks of a river then as now called the Blackwater, in the heart of Meath.

But before the Dedannans themselves ever saw it, the Green Isle was held by the Firbolgs, a terrible, heroic race, but allied to the dark powers. Some say they became demons, after they were defeated in many battles by the Tuatha-De-Danann, and at last wholly conquered. But so old is this ancient tired world, that long before the Dedannans and the Firbolg people fought for sovereignty, the Firbolg had striven with and overcome an earlier race—the Nemedians—which had come to Ireland under a mysterious king, Nemed. None knows who Nemed was, though he may have been a god, seeing that he overcame that most ancient people who were the first to set foot in the Isle of Destiny, under Partholan, a son of him who was called the Most High God.

Whether it be true or not that the overlordship of the world was meant for man, certain it is that man has thought so. Therefore are all stories of his cosmic strife coloured by this destiny. Terrible and mighty were the Firbolgs, fierce and terrible and beautiful were the Dedannans, but now there is no rumour of either, save in the wail of the wind, or in the stirring of swift, stealthy feet in the moonshine.

But now, Peterkin, I will tell you about the children of Lir, who was one of the great princes of the Dedannans.

The first great battle between the Milesians and the Dedannans had been fought, and the ancient people, for all their secret powers of wonders and enchantment, had been defeated. Throughout all Erin—for Ireland at that time was called either Eiré (Erin), or Fola, or Banba, after three great queens—there was a rumour of lamentation. It was the beginning of the end, though few save the wisest Druids foresaw it.

But the people knew that their dissensions were the cause of their sorrow. They clamoured for one king to be overlord, so that the whole Dedannan race might be united.

There were five great princes who claimed to be king by right. Of these two were greater than the others—Bove Derg, son of Dagda, one of the divine race (and some say a mighty god), and Lir of Shee Finnaha. In the end Bove Derg was elected Ardree, or High King. Even Midir the Haughty acquiesced in this judgment of the people, but Lir was wroth and held aloof. All the princes and warriors were fierce with Lir because he had left the assembly in anger, paying heed to no one, and scornfully ignoring the majesty of the king. A hundred swords of proven heroes leapt before Bove Derg, for all were eager to follow Lir and destroy him and his, because of the insult to the king and to the voice and freewill of the people. But Bove Derg was a wise and generous prince, and forbore. This was well. For in time a great sorrow came upon Lir. When the rumour of this sorrow reached Bove Derg, he saw how he might win over Lir.

"In my house," he said, "are my three foster-children, the daughters of Aileel of Ara. Each is beautiful, all are wise and sweet and noble. Let messengers go to Lir, and tell him that my friendship is his if he will have it. Surely now he will submit to the will of the people. And he can have to wife whomsoever of the three daughters of Aileel he may choose, if so be that she will gladly and freely go with him."

Lir was glad at this message.  He called his warriors together, and in fifty chariots he and they set forth.  They rested not till they came to the palace of Bove Derg, by the Great Lake, nigh to the place now called Killaloe.  Great were the rejoicings, and again at the alliance which after many days was made between the king and Lir.

When Lir saw the three daughters of Aileel, he could not say who was the most beautiful.

"Each is alike beautiful, O king," he said ; "and I cannot tell which is best.  But surely the eldest must be the noblest of the three, and so I will choose her, if so be that she gladly and freely come with me as my wife."

And so it was.  When Lir returned to his own place, he took with him as his wife the beautiful Aev, who was the eldest of the daughters of Aileel of Ara, and was foster-child of Bove Derg the king.  From that day, too, a deep and true friendship lived between Bove Derg and Lir.

In the course of time Aev bore him twin children, a son and a daughter.  The daughter was named Fionula, because of her lovely whiteness, and the son was named Aed, for that his eyes, and the mind behind his eyes, were bright and wonderful as a flame of fire.

And at the end of the second year Aev again bore twin children. Both were sons, and they were named Fiachra and Conn. But in giving them life she lost her own.

Lir was in bitter distress because of her death, and for the reason that his four little children were now motherless. He was comforted by Bove Derg, who not only gave him friendship and kingly aid and counsel, but said that he should not be left alone to mourn, and that his little ones should not go motherless.

Thus it was that Aeifa, the second of the daughters of Aileel of Ara and foster-child of Bove Derg the king, came to Shee Finnaha and espoused Lir.

For some years all went well. Aeifa nursed the children, and tended them. They were so fair and beautiful that the poets sang of them far and wide. Even Bove Derg loved them as though they were his own. As for Lir, so great was his love, that he could not bear to be long apart from them. His sleeping-room was separated from them only by a deer-skin, and this often he pulled aside at dawn, so that he might see his dear ones, and perchance go to them to talk lightly and happily, or to caress them with loving laughter and joy.

Lir was never sad save when the four children went south to the Great Lake to stay awhile with Bove Derg, who in his turn was filled with melancholy when the time came for them to go home again. Nor was Lir ever so proud as when, at the Feast of Age, whenever that festival came to be held at Shee Finnaha, the king and the nobles and the warriors delighted in the beauty and marvellous sweet charm of Fionula and Aed and Fiachra and Conn. Thus it was that the saying grew: "Fair as the four children of Lir."

But there was a deep shadow behind all this joy. This shadow came out of the heart of Aeifa. In love there is sometimes a poisonous mist. It is what we call Jealousy. At first Aeifa truly loved her step-children. But as the years lapsed, and when Fionula was passing from girlhood into maidenhood, the wife of Lir was filled with anger against the four children. She was bitter at heart because their father loved them with so great a tenderness, and that even the king himself cared for them above all else, and because all the Dedannans had joy of them.

The time came when this dull smouldering fire, which she might have overcome had she loved nobly and not ignobly, burst into flame. This flame withered her heart, and rose thence till it obscured her mind.

She had something of the old druidical wisdom, but she feared the counter-spells of others wiser than herself. Nevertheless she set herself to learn one or other of the ancient incantations against which even the gods are powerless to avert evil from men and women.

While she was brooding thus—and for weeks and even months she lay in the house of Lir as one stricken with some terrible ill— her rage grew till she could no longer endure the sight of her husband or of her step-children.

One day she arose and ordered the horses to be yoked to her chariot, and bade a small chosen company to be ready to go with her and the four children to the Great Lake : for, she said, she wished to see Bove Derg, her foster-father, and to take the children to gladden his heart. Lir was sad, and sadder still when he saw the tears in Fionula's eyes. In vain he asked her why this drifting dew was

there instead of the sun-bright laughing glanc-
ings he joyed so much to see. She would not
answer : for all she could have said was that
in a dream she had fore-knowledge of the evil
desire of Aeifa to kill her and her brothers.
Perhaps, she thought, it was but a dream.
She loved honour, too, and would not put her
father against his wife because of a visionary
thing that came to her in the night.

It was when they were in a deep gorge of the
hills that Aeifa was overcome by her hatred.
Turning to her attendants, she offered them
wealth and whatsoever they desired if only
they would slay the four children of Lir then
and there, inasmuch as these had come between
her and her husband, and had therein and in
all else made her life a burden to her.

The attendants listened with horror. Not
one there would lift a hand against Lir's children. What was wealth, or any fruit of desire,
compared with so foul a treachery, so terrible a
crime! The oldest among them even warned
Lir's wife that the very thought of such evil
would surely work a dreadful punishment
against her.

At this, Aeifa laughed wildly. Then,
seizing a sword, she strove to wield it herself

against the defenceless children. The three boys stood, wondering. In the blue eyes of Fionula there was something the wife of Lir dreaded more than the wrath of husband or king. Dashing the sword to the ground, she cried to the chariot-driver to make haste onward.

No word was spoken among them till they reached the hither end of the Lake of Darvra.[1] There Aeifa called a halt, and the horses were unyoked for rest. It was a fair and warm day, so when she bade the children undress and go into the water, they did so gladly.

While their white sunlit bodies were splashing in the lake, she took from beneath the rim of the chariot, where she had secreted it, a druidical fairy wand. This had been given her by a Dedannan druid, and was a dreadful thing to possess, for its power was of the black magic, against which nothing might prevail. Going to the side of the clear water, she struck lightly with the wand the shoulder of each of the four children ; and, as she touched Fionula, Lir's fair young daughter became a beautiful snow-white swan, and as she touched Aed and

---

[1] Now Loch Derravaragh, in West Meath.

Fiachra and Conn, Lir's three young sons were changed like unto Fionula.

A cry of lamentation arose from the witnesses of this deed, though none guessed that the ill was so dreadful and beyond the reach of druidic skill, nor did the children know at first what evil had befallen them, but swam to and fro laughing in their hearts, and rejoicing in their white feathers and in their swift joy in the water. But when Fionula heard the lamentation, and looked upon the evil face of Aeifa her stepmother, she knew that the hour of doom had come.

Then Aeifa stretched out her arms, and chanted these words :

" Lost far and wide on Darvra's gloomy water,
   With other lonely birds tost far and wide.
For nevermore shall Lir behold his daughter,
   And never shall his sons lie by his side."

Then while all on the shore stood in deep grief, Fionula swam close, and looked up into the white face of Aeifa, which was whiter then than the whitest breast-feathers of these poor bewildered swans.

" This is an evil deed thou hast done, O Aeifa," she said. " Out of a bitter heart thou hast wrought this cruel wrong upon us who love thee, and have never done or wished thee ill. Nevertheless it is not our ill that shall endure for ever, but thine own evil. There shall be an avenging terrible for thee, whensoever it come."

It was then that Fionula for the first time sang as a swan, and even then the marvellous sweet singing brought both gladness and tears into the hearts of those who heard.

"In the years long ago, long ago now, long ago,
  We were loved by her who dooms us to this evil cruel
      woe :
          Who with magic wand and words
          Hath changed us into birds—
  Snow-white swans to drift and drift for evermore
  Homeless, weary, tempest-baffled hence from shore to
      shore."

A silence followed this melancholy singing. Then at last Fionula spoke again.

" Tell us, O Aeifa, how long this doom is to be upon us, so that we may know when death shall come to take away our suffering ?"

Then because in that day it was not honourable to refuse the truth when asked, Aeifa did as Fionula prayed of her.

" Better would it be for thee and thy brothers to know nothing and to hope much. But since thou hast asked this thing I will tell it :

" Three hundred years shall ye, Fionula, and Aed and Fiachra and Conn, who are now four white swans, abide here on this great lonely, desolate lake of Darvra.  For three hundred years thereafter shall ye inhabit the wild sea of Moyle, which lies between the Stairway of the Giants, and the bleak shores of the great headland of Alba.[1]  And for yet another three hundred years ye shall drift to and fro among the storm-swept seas off the rocky isles to the west of Erin.

" Furthermore, ye shall be idle sport for the storms until Lairgnen, a great prince of the north, has union with Decca, in the south : until the Taillkenn,[2] the new prophet, shall come to Erin and preach a new faith that shall chase away the old gods : and until ye shall be filled with fear and wonder at a strange sound, that shall be the ringing of the first Christian bell.  All this I tell ye because of the prophetic sight I have, and that has come to me

----

[1] That is, between the north-east of Ireland (the Giant's Causeway) and the south-west of the Scottish Highlands (the Mull of Cantire).

[2] The Tailcen : a name given by the early Irish to St. Patrick.

through the druidic wand wherewith I have changed ye into four wild white swans. And this too, I say unto ye, Fionula and Aed and Fiachra and Conn, that neither by your own power nor by your prayers, nor by mine, nor by the power of Lir and Bove Derg, nor by that of all kings and princes and druids whatsoever; no, nor by any god, nor by any power in heaven or earth, can ye be freed from this spell I have put upon ye, until the times and events I have spoken of shall be fulfilled."

When Aeifa had ceased speaking, there was no sound to be heard, save the lap-lapping of the lake-water upon the shore. Of the company of those with her none spake a word, each dreading the evil that was sure to come. At last a faint sobbing came from amid the sedges, where the young brothers nestled by the side of Fionula, who had already begun to mother these dear ones whom she loved.

When she heard these sobs, Aeifa's heart smote her. Even if she would, she could not now undo the age-long spell she had set upon the children of Lir. But one thing was left to her that she might do with the fairy wand, which could be moved once again if stirred by the breath of her will.

"Hearken, O children of Lir," she cried, "for I have yet one thing to say: and that out of the sorrow in my heart because of the doom I have put upon ye. Although ye are turned into wild swans, ye shall not become as the desert birds, and have no speech but the savage screams and cries of the wilderness. Ye shall keep for ever your own sweet Gaelic speech, and so be able to talk each with the other, and with any of the human kind whom ye may meet. And more than this, ye shall be able to sing the most sweet, plaintive songs, and the most wild, haunting music that ever man has heard; so that all whose ears list shall be lulled into deep sleep, or into a peace sweeter than slumber itself. Nor shall the law of the soulless brutes be upon you, but ye shall be Fionula and Aed and Fiachra and Conn, the children of Lir."

Having said these words, Aeifa raised her arms and chanted this song:

> "Speed hence, speed hence, O lone white swans,
>   Across the wind-sprent foam;
> The wave shall be your father now,
> And the wind alone shall kiss your brow,
>   And the waste be your home.

Speed hence, speed hence, O lone white swans,
  Your age-long quest to make;
Three hundred years on Moyle's wild breast,
Three hundred years on the wilder west,
  Three hundred on this lake.

Speed hence, speed hence, O lone white swans,
  And Lir shall call in vain;
For all his aching heart and tears,
For all the weariness of his years,
  Ye shall not come again.

Speed hence, speed hence, O lone white swans,
  Till the ringing of Christ's bell;
Then at the last ye shall have rest,
And Death shall take ye to his breast
  At the ringing of Christ's bell."

Having sung this farewell song, Aeifa ordered the horses to be yoked again to her chariot.

This done, she drove away westward, nor was there a single heart in those who accompanied her but was filled with sorrow and foreboding.

When the lake was no longer visible, and the gloom of the mountains came down upon the pass which led towards the westlands where Bove Derg dwelled, a faint wild aerial singing was heard, delicate as tinkling cow-bells on far hill-pastures.

Before Aeifa drew near to the great dun of Bove Derg, she put each of her company under a solemn bond of silence as to what she had meant to do and not done, and as to what later she had done; and because of the lealty of the bond to a woman, and also because of the fear of each towards the druidical fairy wand that she still carried, the oath was taken by one and all.

Therefore it was easy for Aeifa to mislead Bove Derg as to the reason why she had not brought the children of Lir with her. Nevertheless he doubted greatly that his foster-daughter deceived him, for he could not think that Lir his friend would so mistrust him as to refuse to let Fionula and her brothers accompany their stepmother.

So, secretly, he sent a swift messenger across the hills and straths to the dun of Lir.

Lir was at once wroth and filled with fear when he heard that Aeifa had reached the dun of Bove Derg without the children. Some treachery surely had been done, he cried.

Then, calling together a company, he set forth with all speed. Towards sundown, the cavalcade came upon the wide desolate shores of the great lake of Darvra.

"What is that sound?" cried Lir.

"It is the wind in the reeds, O Lir," answered a spearman by his side.

"The wind in the reeds is a sweet sound to hear, Coran, but never have I heard any wind that could make so sweet a music."

"It is the little gentle lapping of the wavelets by the west wind, O Lir."

"It is no gentle lapping of the wavelets by the west wind, Coran, nor yet is it the wind in the reeds; but that is the voice of Fionula singing."

And as the sound grew clearer, all heard it, and soon the words were audible:

> "Behold the Danann host is on the shore,
> Seeking for those now lost for evermore;
> But let us haste towards that proud array
> And tell the tidings of this fatal day."

And while the song was still in the ears of all there, Lir gave a great cry and pointed to where above the midmost of the lake four wild swans were winging swiftly towards the eastern shore.

When he heard from Fionula—and he knew

her voice, which was sweeter than any other
he had ever heard—of all that had happened,
and of the strange and dreadful doom that
was put upon her and her brothers, he fell
sobbing to the ground.    From all his company the keening of a bitter lamentation
arose.

Alas, as he knew well, not even the great
length of years which the Dedannan folk lived
—and a score of years is to them what one
year is to us—would enable him to see his
dear ones again.    Three hundred years on
Darvra, these he might mayhap live to see;
but not the three hundred years on the bleak
and wild region of the Moyle, nor the three
hundred on the wild tempestuous western seas,
nor the far-off day when a prophet called
Taillken would come to Erin with a new faith,
and in the glens and across the plains would
be heard the strange chiming of Christ's
bell.

Yet was he comforted when he heard that
his children were to keep their Gaelic speech,
and to be human in all things save only in
their outward shape.    And glad he was that
they were to be able to chant music so wild
and sweet that all who should hear it would

be filled with joy and peace. For music is the most beautiful and wonderful thing in the world, and is the oldest, as it will be the latest speech.

"Remain with us this night, here by the lake," said Fionula, "and we shall sing to you our fairy music."

So all abode there, and so sweet was the song of the children of Lir, that he himself and all his company fell into a deep, restful slumber. All night long they sang their sweet sad song, and were glad because of the quiet dark figures by the lake-side, lying drowned in shadow. Slowly the moon sank behind the hills. Then the stars glistened whitelier and smaller, and a soft rosy flush came over the mountain crest in the east. Then Lir awoke, and Fionula and Aed and Fiachra and Conn ceased their singing, and spread out their white pinions to the light of a new day, and ruffled their snowy breasts against the frothing that the dawn-wind made upon the lake.

Lir took a harp from one of his followers, and sang a song of farewell to his children. At that singing all awoke, and the heart of each man was heavy because of the doom that had fallen upon the children of Lir.

He sang of the fateful hour when he had taken Aeifa to wife, and of the cruel hardness of her heart, that thus out of jealous rage she could work so great and unmerited evil. And what rest could there be for him, he chanted, since whenever he lay down in the dark he would see his loved ones pictured plain before him : Fionula, his pride and joy ; Aed, so agile and adventurous ; the laughing Fiachra ; and little Conn, with his curls of gold.

Then with a heavy heart indeed Lir went on his way. Before he and his company entered the great pass at the western end of Lough Darvra, he looked back longingly. In the blue space of heaven he saw four white cloudlets drifting idly in a slow circling flight.

"O Fionula," he cried, "O Aed, O Fiachra, O Conn, farewell, my little ones! Well do I know that you have risen thus in high flight so that my eyes may have this last glimpse of you. Nevertheless I will come again soon."

It was a weary journey thence to the dun of Bove Derg, but all weariness was forgotten in wrath against Aeifa.

No sooner had Lir spoken to the king,

no sooner had the king looked at the face of Aeifa as she heard the accusation, than Bove Derg knew that the truth had been told, and that Aeifa was guilty of this cruel wrong. Turning to his foster-daughter, he exclaimed, in the hearing of all:

" This ill deed that thou hast wrought, Aeifa, will be worse for thee than all thou hast put upon the children of Lir.  For in the end they shall know joy and peace, while as long as the world lasts thou shalt know what it is to be lonely and accursed and abhorred."  Then for a brief time Bove Derg brooded.  There was naught in all the world so dreaded in the dim ancient days as the demons of the air, and no doom could be more dreadful than to be transformed into one of those dark and lonely and desperate spirits that make night and desolate places so full of terror.  At last the king rose.  Taking his druidical magic wand, he struck Aeifa with it, and therewith turned her into a demon of the air.  A great cry went up from the whole assemblage as they saw Aeifa spread out gaunt shadowy wings, and struggle as in a sudden anguish of new birth.  The next moment she gave a terrible scream, and flew upward like a swirling eagle, and disappeared among the dark lowering clouds which hung over the land that day.

Thus was it that Aeifa became a demon o the air. Even now her screaming voice may be heard among the wild hills of her own land, on dark windy nights, when tempests break, or in disastrous hours.

But out of a wrong done the gods may work good. So was it with the Dedannans.

For not only Lir, and all his people, but Bove Derg and a great part of the nation assembled by the shores of Lake Darvra, and there pitched their tents, which afterwards grew into a vast rath, wherein the king builded a mighty dun.

For Lir and Bove Derg had vowed that henceforth they would live their years by the shores of Darvra, where they might converse with their dear ones, and where they might listen to the sweet oblivious songs which Fionula and her brothers sang to the easing of the heart, and the silence of all pain and weariness.

But so great was the rumour of this marvel that all Erin heard of it. The Milesians in the south agreed to a long truce of three hundred years ; and came and dwelt in amity with the Dedannans, for they too loved the sweet and wonderful music of the white swans that were the children of Lir.

"Three hundred years yet may we live," said Bove Derg to Lir, "and as I am a king, I swear never to leave the lough of Darvra while the four swans that are thy sons and daughter inhabit it. The heavy years shall pass for us, listening to their beautiful sweet singing ; and therein we shall know peace and joy."

"So be it," said Lir, and he spoke the truth, for in that day the Dedannans lived to a great age ; some say to three hundred, some to five, some to seven hundred years.

The years went by, one after the other, and by tens and by scores, and still Lir and Bove Derg and the Dedannans and Milesians dwelled by the shores of Lake Darvra. For never in the world's history has there been chronicle of so sweet a singing as that of the four children of Lir. All day the swans discoursed lovingly with their father and Bove Derg, and their kith and kin, and all who sought them ; and each night they sang their slow, sweet, fairy music—a music so wonderful and passing sweet, that all who listed to it forgot weariness and pain and bitter memories and the burden of years, and fell into a deep restful slumber, whence they awoke each morrow as though they had drunken overnight of the Fountain of Youth.

The hair of Lir and Bove Derg was long and white, and almost had the Dedannans and the Milesians forgotten their ancient enmity, when a day of the days came whereon Fionula called aside her three brothers.

"Dear brothers," she said, as she looked sadly at the three beautiful white swans, and at the four drifting shadow-swans in the depths of the lake, " dear brothers, do you know that the time has come when we must put away our happiness as a dream that has been dreamed ? For now the three hundred years of our sojourn here are at an end, and at dawn to-morrow we must arise and wing our sad flight across the dear lands of Erin, till we come to the wild and stormy waters of the sea-stream of the Moyle."

Aed and Fiachra and Conn made so loud and bitter lamentation at this that all heard, and soon the whole host that was encamped there filled the region with long keening cries of grief, and a sorrowful mourning strain as of the melancholy wind among the hills.

But once more all were soothed that night into deep slumber and happy peace, because of the slow, sweet, fairy music of the chanting swans.

At dawn, the four swans arose, and with their white pinions circled high above the lake, glittering as they soared into the sunflood as it swept across the summits of the eastern hills.

"Farewell! farewell! farewell!" they chanted, and at that sad sound all the Dedannan host and all the Milesians, headed by Lir and Bove Derg, kneeled along the lake pastures and amid the reeds and sedges.

Then Fionula, as she and her brothers slowly descended in wide-sweeping curves, sang this song :

> " Farewell ! Farewell ! Farewell !
> Far hence we lost ones go :
>     Hearken our knell,
>     Hearken our woe !
>
> Farewell ! Farewell ! Farewell !
> With breaking hearts we flee :
>     For none can tell
>     Our wild home on the sea.

For ages on the Moyle,
In loneliness and pain,
    Our feet shall tread no soil,
    Wild wave, wild wind, wild rain.

For ages in the west,
Fierce storms and fiercer cold
    Shall be alone our rest,
    While ye grow old.

Let not our memories pass,
O ye who stay behind—
    Who are as the grass
    And we the wind.

Farewell! Farewell! Farewell!
Far hence we lost ones go :
    Hearken our knell,
    Hearken our woe !"

As Fionula ceased this song, she and her brothers swept so close to the water's edge that their white wings made a little dazzle of spray. Then with swift pinions they rose again, and soared in great spirals of flight, till they gleamed against the morning blue like four white banners adrift before a skiey wind.

Then for a brief while they suspended on outspread wings, and looked longingly down upon the dear ones and all their kith and kin, who on their part could scarce see the four white swans for the mist of tears that was before all faces.

Suddenly they swung hither and thither, like foam tossed by a tidal wind, and then flew straight to the northward. Soon they were but white specks; then the blue closed in upon them, as the wastes of the sea close at last behind the hulls of drifting ships.

Before the torch of a stormy sun sank that night amid the tossed green billows of the Moyle, there where the sea flows to and fro betwixt Erin and Alba, the children of Lir drooped their weary wings. Their home now was the running wave. In darkness and loneliness and sorrow, they floated close to each other, waiting for the dawn to steal into that first night of bitter exile.

From that day they were severed from those who loved them. Of a truth, there was keening and lamentation and sorrow by the shores of the lough of Darvra. At the last, as the snow melts, the great host of the Dedannans and Milesians passed away: to the westward, some; others, to the south.

As for Bove Derg and Lir, their white hairs and the grey ashes of their lives were the mournful refrain of many a song on the lips of wandering bards.

There were tears in the eyes of Peterkin when Ian Mor ceased speaking. His heart was sore because of Fionula and Aed and Fiachra and Conn.

Nevertheless, he too would be glad to be a swan for a time, if only so as to be able to soar into the blue spaces of the sky, and to spread white wings over the dancing waters, and to move through them swifter than any boat. With what joy he had once climbed on to the fan of an old windmill, and slowly revolved through the hot August air, which winnowed around him a coolness like the flowing of wind over the summit of a hill.

A bright shining came into his eyes, then laughter bubbled to his lips.

Eilidh looked at him, half in mock reproof, half rejoicingly.

" Peterkin, why do you laugh ? "

" Oh, for sure, dear, it's not laughing I am at the poor swans, but at the face of Old Nanny, my nurse, when she came out of the cottage in the glen and saw me lying flat and holding on to the fan of the windmill, with my hair all blown back, and both my legs hanging in the air."

" Some day you will kill yourself, Peterkin," said Eilidh gravely.

" Then I'll be a swan ! and I'll fly round and round Iona, and whenever you or Ian want to go to the mainland, I'll take you on my back."

Suddenly Peterkin sprang to his feet, and jumped to and fro, clapping his hands.

" Ah, how I would love it !" he exclaimed.

" Love what, dearie ?"

" Love to see Ian fall off my back and go plump in among the herrings in the Sound ! *What* a splash he would make !"

" And poor Ian—— Why, he might be drowned, Peterkin !"

"Oh, no ; I would swoop down the way a gannet does when it sees a fish, and would scoop him up with my bill."

The picture was too much for Peterkin. The thought of grabbing the dripping half-drowned Ian in his bill, and of soaring away with him to the white dry sands, was better than any dream of the fairies he had ever had, even than that when he rode a fairy horse in the guise of a white mouse, with grasshoppers

for hounds, and a great bumble-bee as a wild
boar for the occasion.  He threw himself on
the floor in front of the hearth, and rolled
over and over, contorting his small body into
alarming convulsions, clapping his hands, and
laughing, laughing, laughing.

Eilidh, too, let the laughter take her, and
then Ian found it sweet ; and soon the little
room was full of joyous laughter upon laughter,
and of the leaping flame-light from the blazing
log on the peats, and of the dancing of the
shadow-men in the corners and up and down
the walls.

"The swans!  The swans!" cried Peterkin
suddenly, as he grabbed wildly at some shadowy
shapes which slid along the floor.  But these
swans proved as tantalising as the wind-
shadows on the grass which so often he chased,
and suddenly in a flash they disappeared altogether.  They seemed to spring right into Ian
Mor ; at any rate it was in his arms that Peterkin found himself.

"Where are the shadows ?  Where are the
shadows, Ian ?" he cried : "I believe you are
hiding them inside yourself!  Where are they ?
Where are they ?"

"Why, you boykin, where could they be ?"

" They are in your heart, Ian !   I know they are !   I see them !   I see them !"

Ian glanced at Eilidh.   Then, putting his arm round Peterkin, he laid his lips against his downy cheek and whispered :

" Yes, my little lad, you've guessed right."

"Then why don't you chase them out, Ian ?"

Again Ian Mor glanced at Eilidh.

"They live there, lennavan-mo.   They jumped out because of your laughter, but they are back now."

" Then I'll be laughing often, Ian dear, and some day I'll catch them and drive them out into the sunshine, and then they'll melt—ay, ay, they'll melt for sure, Ian, and what will you be after doing then ? "

" Well, like Fionula and the wild swans, Peterkin, I'll rise up and soar away on the great flood of the sun across the sea till I come to Hy Brásil, the Isle of Youth far away in the West."

" Yes, I know," Peterkin said gravely : " Hy Brásil : Eilidh told me that is where she and you are going to live.   Will you take me there too ? "

" Yes, you will come there too, mochree, some day."

"But with you — when you and Eilidh go?"

"Perhaps we'll not be going there together, Peterkin.   But we won't be forgetting our dear little Peterkin.   We'll be on the shore looking out for you when you come."

"Why are your eyes wet, Ian, and Eilidh's too?"

"Why, you unfeeling little wretch, it's because we have left the poor swans, Fionula, and Aed, and Fiachra, and Conn, alone on the rough seas of the Moyle all this while."

"Tell me, tell me now about the children of Lir.   Did they see any one up there?   Were they ever happy?"

"Eilidh knows the rest of the story as well as I do, Peterkin, so go and sit in her lap while she tells it to you and to me."

With that, Ian Mor rose and put another log on the red peats.   A shower of sparks shot up into the dark hollow of the chimney.   Peterkin laughed.

"Hush!" whispered Eilidh, with smiling eyes : and then in her sweet, low voice resumed the tale of the Children of Lir, from where Ian had stopped.

It was at the edge of winter when Fionula and her brothers reached the wild bleak seas of the Moyle.

At first there was no too bitter cold or too fierce tempestuousness to make their evil lot still more hard to bear ; but sad indeed were their hearts as day after day they saw nothing but the same grey skies, the same grey wastes and dark sullen waves, the same bleak, rocky coasts inhabited only by the cormorant and the sea-mew. Never to see a familiar face, never to hear a familiar voice : to dwell from morning dusk till evening dark in loneliness and sorrow —that, indeed, was a hard fate upon the four children of Lir. From hunger and cold, too, they suffered much. No longer could they be cheered as they were on Lough Darvra, and often and often they lamented that their doom could not have permitted them to remain as swans indeed, but as swans on that now dear and home-sweet inland sea of Darvra.

Day after day passed, but while their misery and want did not grow less they were not yet tortured by wintry storms and bitter frosts.

But one forlorn afternoon a terrible congregation of clouds, black and heavy and flanked with livid gleams, appeared above the horizon and slowly invaded the whole west, and then all the sky northward and all southward.

Fionula saw that a great tempest was nigh, so she called Aed, and Fiachra, and Conn, to come to her side.

" Dear brothers," she exclaimed, " the storm that will soon be upon us will be worse than any we have yet known.  Hardly can we hope not to be driven far apart.  Let us agree, therefore, to meet somewhere, if so be that we are not utterly destroyed.  For though Aeifa, our cruel stepmother, doomed us to these long ages of suffering, it may well be that even her potent spell is not strong enough against death : and death may come to us through famine, or cold, or in the drowning wave."

At first the brothers could answer nothing. Then Aed spoke.  " Thou art wise, dear Fionula.  Let us, then, fix upon the rocky isle of Carrick-na-ron, as that place is well known to each of us, and can be descried from a great way off."

Thus it was that Carrick-na-ron was made their place of meeting, if so be that in the blind fury and confusion of the tempest they should be driven the one from the other.

This was well : for that night, with the darkening of the night into a hollow of starless blackness, a terrible tempest swept over the seas, and lashed them into foam and into vast heaving, rolling, swaying billows. Amid the noise of the waves, and behind the screaming of the wind, the four weary rain-drenched bewildered swans could hear the crashing of the thunder and see the wild fitful blue glare of savage lightnings.

Before midnight they were whirled this way and that by the fierce paws of the gale. Soon they were separated, and with despairing cries, each swept solitary through the night. In the heart of each of the children of Lir there was little hope of any morrow. All nearly died of weariness and despair. Nevertheless dawn broke at last, and with the first coming of light the tempest passed away.

When the sun rose the waters were almost smooth again. A sparkling came into the crest of every wave. The sea blued.

Fionula was the first to descry the rocky isle of Carrick-na-ron, and gladly she swam towards it, for she was now too weary to fly. Eagerly she hoped to find her brothers there, safe-havened. Alas, there was not a sign of any, not even when she flew to the summit of the highest rock and looked far and wide across the wilderness of waters.

Great sorrow was hers, for sure, when she beheld nothing but wave upon wave, wave upon wave, till on the far horizon the long low line of sea climbed into the sky.

A song of mourning broke from Fionula, so sad and sweet and despairing that the gannets and sea-mews and dark fierce cormorants wheeled around Carrick-na-ron, wondering at the marvel of this wild swan, with the strange remote voice of the human kind. It was a song of farewell.

When Fionula ceased her lament she looked once more across the wastes of the sea. Suddenly she uttered a glad cry, for she descried Conn swimming slowly towards the rocky isle, slowly, and with drooping head, for he was drenched with the salt brine, and so weary that he could scarce move.

Hardly had she welcomed him with joy, and helped him to reach a flat ledge of rock whereon the sunlight poured with healing warmth, than she saw Fiachra desperately striving to make his way towards them, but so far spent that it seemed as though death would overtake him before he reached the foam-edged rocks. Fionula sprang into the running wave, and soon was beside Fiachra, aiding him to her utmost. With difficulty she helped him to the ledge where Conn crouched in the sun, but so weak was he that when he was spoken to he could utter no word in reply. Fionula looked with pity upon her two young brothers. It was hard for her to see their unmothered pain and weariness. So she spread out her broad white pinions, and gave the warmth of her body to the two drenched and shivering swans.

"Ah!" she exclaimed, as she crouched on the ledge, with Fiachra nestling by her right side and Conn by her left; "ah! if only Aed were here too, all might yet be well. And even if it be death, sweeter far that we might all perish together." It was as though her loving prayer were answered, for before long she descried Aed swimming swiftly through the sunny foam-splashed seas. He, at least, she saw with joy, had not suffered as his younger brothers had done, for he came on with head erect and his white plumage all unruffled and dazzlingly ashine.

Nevertheless, Aed, too, was glad to rest in the sunshine, so Fionula placed him under her breast.

Noon found them thus: Fionula with sad eyes staring out across the wastes of windy seas; under the warm feathers of her breast, Aed; and close nestled to the warm down of her sides, Fiachra and Conn.  She heard their low breathing as they slept, and that they might sleep the deeper and longer she sang her low, sweet, fairy music:

Sleep, sleep, brothers dear, sleep and dream,
Nothing so sweet lies hid in all your years.
Life is a storm-swept gleam
In a rain of tears:
Why wake to a bitter hour, to sigh, to weep?
How better far to sleep——
To sleep and dream.

To sleep and dream, ah, that is well indeed:
Better than sighs, better than tears;
Ye can have nothing better for your meed
In all the years.
Why wake to a bitter hour, to sigh, to weep?
How better far to sleep——
To sleep and dream, ah, that is well indeed!

This and other songs Fionula chanted low throughout the day, till at last she too was overcome by her weariness; and she slept.

At the rising of the moon, all awoke.  Full glad were Aed and Fiachra and Conn that their tribulation was over; only Fionula knew that the doom which Aeifa had put upon them held worse things, and many, in store for them.

For some days thereafter there was peace. Then a snow-whisper came, and the inland hills and the peaked summits of the isles were white. The cold grew deeper day by day; at each dawn the frost bit with a keener grip. The bitter hardships of the children of Lir were now more almost than they could bear. Nevertheless, they had a yet more dreadful trial to endure: for at mid-winter there came a tempest of whirling snow and icy wind so fierce and terrible, that for a day and a night the waves were strewn with the dead bodies of sea-mews and terns. Nothing the four swans had ever suffered was like unto what they suffered at this time.

But when Fionula had again found and sheltered her dear ones, and mothered them with her great love, she knew that whatever their sufferings they would now surely endure until the end. Had they been subject to the mortal law, they could not have survived that dreadful day, and still more awful night.

And so another year passed. The worst sorrow of the children of Lir was their great loneliness, a thing more bitter than hunger or thirst or any privation. They longed for their kind as the first white flowers of the year long for the sun. When mid-winter came again a terrible frost arose. All the north isles were like black bosses in a gleaming shield, for sheets of ice covered the seas, and each island was gripped as in an iron vice. Day by day the cold grew more terrible. On the morrow of the ninth day the four children of Lir thought that the end of their misery was at hand. The whole sea was one solid floor of ice ; the isle of Carrick-na-ron, where they were, was like a black iceberg ; into ice lapsed each faint failing breath that they drew with ever greater pain.

Each morning they had waked to find their feet frozen to the rock, and even the edges of their wings ; and a bitter thing it was to tear themselves free, and to leave clinging to the rock the soft feathers of their breasts and the outer quills of their wings and the skin of their feet.

How fain each was of death! How gladly they would have passed away from the world of the living, though in exile, and longing with aching hearts to see once more their own dear land and the faces of those whom they loved!

But their doom was on them, and they could not leave the sea of Moyle, nor could they win death.

The brave heart of Fionula knew this. She knew too what cruel pain it would give her and her brothers to swim through the salt seas with their bleeding wounds, for the brine would enter them and cause agony. Nevertheless, she led them forth towards the coast of the mainland. There they found a fjord and a haven amid the pine-clad shores, and before long their wounds were healed, and the feathers on their wings and breasts grew again.

But of what avail to tell the tale of all their years? Fionula saw that while they must ever return each night to the sea of Moyle till the three hundred years were over and done, they might fly as far and wide as they could between dawn and dusk. Mighty and strong were they now upon the wing, and fit to endure the slashing of rains, the buffetings of wild winds, the whirling briny sleet of the seas, and the cold of the high forlorn spaces of the lonely sky.

Far and wide therefore they roamed, sometimes along the foam-swept headlands of Alba, sometimes by the stormy coasts of Erin, sometimes for leagues and leagues out into the vast dim wilderness, wherein, so men said, Hy Brásil lay—Hy Brásil, the Isle of Rest, the Isle of Joy, the Isle of Youth Eternal.

One day, far in the oblivion of these self-same years, they chanced to be flying past the mouth of the Bann, on the north coast of Erin : and Aed gave a cry of joy, and bade Fionula and his brothers look inland, for there, coming out of the south-west, was a stately cavalcade, the horsemen mounted on white steeds, beautifully apparelled, and with weapons gleaming in the sun.

How joyous it was to see their own kind again ! All gave a cry of rapture, their hearts aching the while that they could not set foot upon the land, as that was forbidden to them, though they might adventure to the shore.

Long and earnestly Fionula looked, but she could not tell who the strangers were.

" Keen are your eyes, Aed," she said ; " can you discern who the men of yonder cavalcade are ? "

" I know them not as men : but it seems to me that they are a troop of our own Dedannan folk, or perchance they may be of the Milesians."

But while they were still wondering and discussing, the cavalcade drew nearer, and the men of it saw the four swans, and, recognising them as the children of Lir, made signs to Fionula and her brothers to alight on the shore.

With joy the Dedannans, for so they were, hailed the poor exiles, for whom indeed they had long been seeking along the north coasts of Erin. As for the children of Lir they could scarce speak, so great was their happiness to hear their dear familiar speech once more and to see the faces of their own people.

Again and again they were embraced by the two chiefs of the Fairy Host, as the Dedannan warriors were called—Aed the keen-witted, and Fergus the chess-player, the two sons of Bove Derg, king of the Tuatha-De-Danann.

With joy the children of Lir learned that their father was still alive, and was even then celebrating at his house at Shee Finnaha, along with Bove Derg and the chiefs of the Dedannans, the Feast of Age. As for Aed and Fergus and all their following, they wept when they heard the tale of the misery of these lost years, when Fionula and Aed and Fiachra and Conn were the sport of the winds.

While eagerly and lovingly they were conversing, none noticed that the sun was sinking upon the low wavering line of the ultimate wave. But when at last Fionula saw this, she uttered a sad cry of warning to her brothers, and all four rose on their white wings and made ready to fly back to the bleak and desolate sea of Moyle. And sad, sadder than ever, was the heart of Fionula, for she knew that they could not be there till nightfall, and that the penalty of this would be that they should not again see the face of their kind, either on the shores of Erin or Alba, until the end of the three hundred years on the wastes of the Moyle.

As they circled in the air, she sang this song, the last of the swan-songs heard of any of the Dedannans who were in that company :

> Happy our father Lir afar,
> With mead, and songs of love and war :
> The salt brine, and the white foam,
> With these his children have their home.
>
> In the sweet days of long ago
> Soft-clad we wandered to and fro :

But now cold winds of dawn and night
Pierce deep our feathers thin and light.

The hazel mead in cups of gold
We feasted from in days of old:
The sea-weed now our food, our wine
The salt, keen, bitter, barren brine.

On soft warm couches once we pressed
While harpers lulled us to our rest:
Our beds are now where the sea raves,
Our lullaby the clash of waves.

Alas! the fair sweet days are gone
When love was ours from dawn to dawn:
Our sole companion now is pain,
Through frost and snow, through storm and rain.

Beneath my wings my brothers lie
When fierce the ice-winds hurtle by:
On either side and 'neath my breast
Lir's sons have known no other rest.

Ah, kisses we shall no more know,
Ah, love so dear exchanged for woe,
All that is sweet for us is o'er,
Homeless for aye from shore to shore.

A great lamentation went up from the cavalcade of the Fairy Host when Fionula ended
this song, and she and her brothers · flew
swiftly northward athwart the waves, red and
wild because of the stormy setting of the sun.

Sad was the tale the Dedannans had to relate when they returned to Shee Finnaha.

Nevertheless, Bove Derg, the aged king, and white-haired Lir himself, took comfort in this, that Fionula and her brothers were still alive. Moreover, they knew that in the end the spell of Aeifa would be broken and that the exiles would be freed from their sufferings.

But often, often, they thought with tears, as the slow revolving seasons lapsed one into the other, of the children of Lir upon the desolate far seas of the Moyle.

Here Eilidh's voice lapsed into silence. Then, looking no longer at Peterkin, but staring into the red heart of the peats, she sang a Gaelic song, called the Sorrow of the Grey Hairs of Lir.

Peterkin never loved Eilidh so well as when she sang ; but he was sorrowful to-night when he saw that the song brought tears into her eyes.

" Eilidh," he whispered.

" Yes, Peterkin, dear."

" Wouldn't you be liking to kiss Ian ?"

Eilidh laughed low, a faint flush coming and going upon her face.

"For why, boykin ?"

"Oh, I know that whenever you have tears in your eyes Ian can chase them away. I have seen him kiss you when you are tired."

At this Ian Mor rose and lifted Peterkin in his arms.

"Eilidh is thinking of something sad, Peterkin ; that is all. See, she is smiling now, and laughing too by the same token." The boy tossed his curls, and with a roguish smile added :

"Ah, that is just because I said she wanted to kiss you."

"You're much too wise, Peterkin. But there, down with you! Now run to the door, and tell me if it is still raining."

Peterkin never could go straight anywhere, for his progress was ever like that of a kid or lambkin, a series of jumps and little sudden runs. No sooner was he gone, than Ian turned to Eilidh, and took her in his arms.

"Sweetheart," he whispered, "that little burst o' sunshine is right. A kiss from your lips is the best thing to chase away the tears. But why are you sad, mochree ?"

"I was thinking of the sorrow of old Lir ; and how little it matters whether one live fifty years or five hundred, as these old Dedannans did. Then suddenly the thought flashed across me that some day soon we should lose Peterkin : he too will become a wild swan, and it will be we who shall hear the far-off singing of his laughing childhood."

"Perhaps he will take his childhood with him into manhood, dear. Let him look often into your beautiful eyes, Eilidh, and the little one will learn much without knowing that he is learning. And then, too, to be near you : why, that is to be a child always deep down, and to have sunshine in the heart and mind— for have you forgotten your name, 'Sunshine' ?"

As he spoke, Ian Mor leaned and kissed her. Puzzled at the sudden radiant smile on her face, he looked round. There was Peterkin, sitting squatted on the hearth, with an impish smile in his blue eyes. He had crawled behind the hanging curtain at the door, and unseen and unheard gained the fireside.

With a joyous laugh he sprang to his feet.

"Ah, Ian, you and your rain ! Is it not hearing you are ? It's on the window as if the brownies were throwing little wee stones. It was not the rain you were wanting, but only a kiss from Eilidh! Now, Eilidh, tell me true?"

"Tell you true, Blumpits. Why——"

But here Peterkin, overcome by some sudden memory suggested by the pet name which Eilidh sometimes gave him, went dancing round the room, laughing and chuckling by turns, and once and again clapping his hands in elfin glee.

"Eilidh, Eilidh," he cried, "do tell me again that story of Blumpits and the Bunnywig."

Ian looked puzzled.

"What's a bunnywig, Blumpits?"

"A bunnywig—you're not for knowing what a bunnywig is—and you, Ian Mor, too! A bunnywig is a *kunak*."[1]

"And what did Blumpits do?"

"He got on the bunnywig, in the green fern, and rode on it into fairyland, and no one saw him go but a squirrel. But no, Eilidh, I am not wanting to hear about that now ; and don't be looking at my bed there, for I haven't got the sleep upon me yet. Tell me the rest of

[1] Coineag, Gaelic for "rabbit." The common English equivalent, Bunny, is a Gaelic derivative, from *Bun*, a stump or tail.

the tale about Fionula and Aed and Fiachra and Conn."

" I wonder, now, if that's because you really want to hear, or if it's because you don't want to be sent to bed ?".

Peterkin had kicked aside his shoes, and taken off his socks, and was warming his feet at the fire.  His body was bent nearly double, as he looked round, clutching the while his big toe in the hollow of his tiny fist.

" O Eilidh," he said reproachfully, but with a light of such mischief in his eyes that Eilidh laughed.  Then stooping, she took him on her lap, and after a few seconds, when all three looked idly and dreamily into the red fanwave in the heart of the peats, her lips moved again to the sorrowful sweet tale of the Children of Lir.

Year after year passed for the four swans that were the children of Lir.  On that bleak and lonely sea of the Moyle they saw none of their own kind from year's end to year's end : only the sea-mew and the cormorant, the gannet and the tern, the slow droves of the pollack, the travelling schools of mackerel and herring, the swift seals migrating from isle to isle. With each Spring they saw the great solanders and wild swans flying northward towards the polar seas : thence, at the first days of winter, they saw them again flying southward, athirst for the thin blue wine of unfrozen seas.

There was no change save the changefulness of the seasons ; the grey-black wave of winter lapsed into the grey-blue wave of spring, and out of the dark-blue wave of summer grew the grey-green wave of autumn.

Cold and hunger and weariness : these only did not vary.

But at last the long weary exile on the Sea of Moyle came to an end. One day Fionula told her brothers that on the morrow they would have to fly far westward, for the three hundred years on the sea-stream of the Moyle were over, and now they had to begin their long and mayhap still more bitter, bleak, and mournful exile on the wild western ocean beyond Erin.

"We must fly straight to the bleak headland of Irros Domnann," she said, "and then must remain on the wild and desolate seas off the isle of Glora, the island that is farthest away from the mainland of our beloved Erin."

Thither, accordingly, the four swans flew on the morrow. It was with joy that they left the sea of the Moyle, where they had known so much privation and misery ; but little cause had they for joy, for not less' bleak were the skies, not less desolate the coasts, not less wild the storm-lashed, rain-swept seas, off the lifeless, barren isle of Glora. The great waves of the shoreless western ocean beat upon it for ever, and their thunder often filled the darkness for countless leagues with a sound most dreadful to hear.

But after many years it chanced that a young man, named Ebric, the son of a Dedannan lord, came to farm a tract of land lying along the shore of Irros Domnann. This youth, who was a poet, and loved all beautiful things, soon cared more for the sweet, wonderful singing of the four swans, which often he heard, and to see their white bodies glistening in the sun, than to till his land.

One day Fionula and her brothers descried him. Flying to the shore, they called, and great was his wonder to hear the dear familiar Gaelic speech in the mouths of wild swans.

From that time he walked daily down to the extreme rocks on the shore, that he might converse with the children of Lir, and hear all they had to tell of their sad story ; though he, on his part, could relate little to them of what had happened, or was happening further inland in Erin, though they heard from him with sorrow that the Milesians were now mightier than the Dedannans, and that the Fairy Host was no longer able to withstand the might of these enemies who long since had come out of the south.

"For," he said, "it is the way of what is beautiful and wonderful ; that the wonder passes and the beauty fades."

That night he heard Fionula singing, and knew that the burden of her song was no other than the saying he had uttered :

Dim face of Beauty haunting all the world,
Fair face of Beauty all too fair to see,
Where the lost stars adown the heavens are hurled,
    There, there alone for thee
    May white peace be.

For here where all the dreams of men are whirled
Like sere torn leaves of autumn to and fro,
There is no place for thee in all the world,
    Who driftest as a star,
    Beyond, afar.

Beauty, sad face of Beauty, Mystery, Wonder,
What are these dreams to foolish babbling men —
Who cry with little noises 'neath the thunder
Of ages ground to sand,
To a little sand.

Ebric moved homeward through the moonlight wondering much at that song of Fionula. But because he was a poet, he understood.

From him the people of the hills, and the valleys round about Irros Domnann, heard the story of the speaking swans; and soon the wonder of it, and the whole sorrowful tale of the Children of Lir became as well known in that region as, long, long ago, to the Dedannans and Milesians on the shores of Lough Darvra, when they encamped by its shores because of the slow, sweet, fairy music of the four swans.

Then once again it chanced that the four children of Lir unwittingly transgressed their doom, and so had to leave the shores where they could converse with the people who loved them. But Ebric, to whom they had told everything, was a poet, and wrought of their story a tale so sweet and marvellous that it has lasted all these ages, and is heard to this day on the lips of peasants in the west of Erin.

From that time onward the sufferings of Fionula and her brothers were no less than they had been on the sea of the Moyle. Yet even the worst they had there known was surpassed midway in the heart of a terrible winter, a winter when cattle died in covered sheds, and men and women in their houses, and the wild creatures of the forest under their branches, and the storm-inured seabirds in the hollows of their ocean-fronting cliffs.

On that day the whole surface of the sea from Irros Domnann to Achill was frozen into one solid mass of ice. Across this a polar wind drove sheets of hail and sleet. By nightfall, Aed and Fiachra and Conn were so far spent that they despaired of any morrow; and at the last Fionula herself, who had striven to comfort them, was herself in so pitiful a misery that she could only lament with them that death was so long in coming.

But in the full horror of midnight, while they clung nigh-frozen to the rock of Glora, Fionula had a vision. It was of that God, that new faith, that great wonder and beauty which was even then coming towards Erin, though St. Patrick had not yet set foot upon its shores.

" Brothers," she cried, " take heart. I have

had a vision. Of a truth our ancient gods are but the children of a greater than they. Aed, dear Aed and Fiachra and Conn, believe now in this great and loving God, the most splendid God of the living truth: for it is He who has made all things, the pleasant, fruitful land and the wild barren sea; and it has been revealed to me that if we put our trust in Him, He will comfort us and send us help."

"That we now do, O Fionula!" cried Aed and Fiachra and Conn.

Thereupon they fell into a deep slumber. When they awoke the sun was shining; the fierce wind no longer blew; the waves danced joyously, tossing little sheets of spray from one to another. The bitter cold was gone, and they rejoiced exceedingly.

"It is Spring!" Aed cried, with joy.

"It is the answer of God," said Fionula gravely.

From that hour they had peace. Thenceforth they suffered no more from cold or hunger. When the savage frosts of winter, or the wild rains of autumn, came over the western sea, the four swans alighted on Innis Glora, and sang their wild, sweet, beautiful music, and then fell asleep, nestling side by side, till they awoke to warmth and joy.

So was it till the end of the three hundred years. Three hundred years on the lough of Darvra; three hundred on the sea-stream of the Moyle; three hundred on the sea of Glora, to the west of Erin. All these ages had they endured, and now their exile was at an end.

"On the morrow, dear brothers," Fionula sang rejoicingly, "on the morrow we shall wing our way inland; for our hearts ache to see again our own country and our kindred, and the faces of Lir our father, and Bove Derg the king, and all whom we love. Great shall be the joy at Shee Finnaha when they behold us once more; but not more joyous shall their delight be than it will be for us to see the smoke rising from the fires of our people, and to see the greatness and beauty of Shee Finnaha."

They could not sleep that night for eagerness. At dawn they rose on white wings, circling through the wide blue spaces of the air. When the yellow stream of the sun poured westward out of the mountain-ridges of Achill, they chanted a farewell song, and then stretched their wide pinions and flew homeward with beating hearts.

Sweet it was to see below them the green grass instead of the cold, running wave ; and the hollows of the meadows, how much dearer were they than the troughs of the drowning billows !

When they came to the great hill above Shee Finnaha, their wings were seized with so great a trembling that scarcely could they reach into view of Lir's high shining house.

Descending, therefore, they alit on a rock and rested awhile. A deep sadness oppressed Fionula. There was so great a silence on every rock, on every tree. Moreover, she had seen a stag stand staring inland with idle eyes, and had seen the hill-fox and the wolf prowling in the glen where as a child she had often played.

"What is the fear that is in your eyes, Fionula ? " asked one of her brothers with sudden dread.

"Alas ! Aed, if Lir and the Dedannans were still here, would a stag stand staring inland, where Shee Finnaha is, with heedless eyes and no hoof lifted, and nostrils idly sniffing the unfrequented wind ? "

"Of a surety no, Fionula."

"Yet that have I seen, Aed. And if in Shee Finnaha still dwelled our Dedannan folk, would the hill-fox and the wolf prowl in the Glen of the White Water, there where we were wont to play and bathe, we and all the little children?"

"Of a surety no, Fionula."

"Yet that have I seen, O Aed and Fiachra and Conn. Come! we are rested now. Let us hasten homeward to Shee Finnaha, that we have longed for all these years, and to our father Lir, who awaiteth us."

Onward they flew.

But just as they soared over the shoulder of Knoc-na-Shee, Fionula uttered a piercing cry.

There indeed was the valley where Lir long, long ago had made his home. But now there was not a single wreath of smoke rising to the sky, not a single cow lowed in the pastures, neither man nor woman nor child moved to and fro. Nay, there were not even any houses. All had gone. Amid the desolate place rose the gaunt, dishevelled ruins of Lir's great dun; its halls empty and roofless, or tenanted only by the rank grass and tall companies of nettles.

"Alas!" cried Aed, "for the omen of the

stag staring idly on Shee Finnaha, and for that of the hill-fox and the wolf prowling in the Glen of the White Water."

But Fionula could speak no word, for her heart was breaking.

For long they crouched silent amid the desolation of that ruined place. Thrice three hundred years had passed since they had played in front of the house of Lir: beneath yonder ruined wooden arch they had set forth with Aeifa on that ill-fated journey.

The dusk came. Still the four children of Lir crouched silent amid the ruined desolation which was all that remained of lordly Shee Finnaha.

The wolf prowled near, but turned away the flame of his yellow eyes, for he feared those who crouched there and had the voices of the human kind. The bats and owls alone paid no heed.

When the stars glistened in the sky, and the moon rose, and on the night wind there was not the lowing of a cow or the barking of a dog, or any sound whatsoever, save from the rustling forest and the murmuring stream, Fionula and Aed and Fiachra and Conn fell into a bitter sobbing and a long, mournful keen, that rose into the hills with plaintive echoes.

When the day broke, each told the other that they could no longer stay in Shee Finnaha. That desolation was now to them more bitter than the wilderness of the bleak seas of the Moyle. While they were still speaking thus sorrowfully, Conn descried an old man—so old and worn that his hair hung about his wrinkled face like thistledown, so white and bleached was it. He carried a small harp, but in his eyes was the look of one who saw only far into the mind and never from the mind outward.

"Who art thou, O stranger?" Conn asked.

The man looked at the swan that spoke to him in human speech, and in the sweet, familiar tongue of the Gael.

"I have heard strange things," he muttered, "and in my madness have come to learn of the beasts. Have not the hawks and eagles of Shee Finnaha told me bitter tidings, and has not the hill-fox barked to me of the graves of dead hopes, and has not the she-wolf whined to me in the dusk of the sorrows that flit through the woods—the old ancient sorrows of the wise and the beautiful and the brave that are now no more? Why then should not a wild swan speak? Have I forgotten that, ages ago, the children of Lir were changed into swans, and that they spoke with the human tongue, and sang songs so passing sweet that life and death became as the self-same dream? Ah! that dream of dreams: fragrant it was as the breath of Moy Mell, the honey-sweet plain of Heaven; restful as the sound of the waves beating on the shores of Tir-fa-Tonn, where the dead dwell in youth and joy; strange and wild as the noise of in-visible wings over the blessed isle that is Hy Brásil in the west."

Conn spake again:

" Art thou a Dedannan, old man ? "

" A Dedannan I am, O Swan, that speakest with the tongue of man; yea, a Dedannan I am, if a sere and fallen leaf can be called a child of the green tree. Say, rather, a De-dannan I was."

" Dost thou know aught of Bove Derg, the King of the Dedannans, or of Lir, the lord of Shee Finnaha ? "

The stranger sighed, and by the veiling of his eyes Conn knew that the old harper was with the past.

"Ay," he muttered at last, "but who can note the passage of the years when one is old and broken and sick unto death? A hundred years have trodden the red leaves again, or it may be thrice a hundred, since I chanted the death-song of Bove Derg, the King of the Dedannans; since I looked on the white face of Lir, as he lay grey and ashy among the ashy-grey thistles."

Conn uttered a cry of sorrow, and a bitter keen of lament came from his two brothers and from Fionula.

"Then these also speak," muttered the old harper : "almost can I persuade myself that I look on the wild swans that are the four children of Lir—Fionula and Aed and Fiachra and Conn. Ages ago I thought they had lapsed in death. All are gone now, save only Aeifa, who is a demon of the air, and wails among the hills and in desolate places."

All this time Fionula had been looking earnestly at the old man. Now she spoke.

"Tell me, art thou not Irbir the Harper?"

"It is Irbir the Harper I am, the chief harper of Bove Derg, that was King of the Dedannans before the Fairy Host faded away from the meadows and pastures of Erin. And if indeed ye be the children of Lir, know I am that Irbir who sang the birth-song at the birthing of ye, Fionula and Aed, and at the birthing of ye, Fiachra and Conn."

Thereupon the old harper embraced the four swans, tears running down his face the while.

While he was yet embracing them, his wildered mind began to wander, and he talked idly of vain things.

Nevertheless, they learned from him that more than a hundred years back, and maybe thrice a hundred, the Tuatha-De-Danann had fought a last great battle with the Milesians and had been utterly defeated. They were now a dispersed and hidden people, some deathless, others living to the thousand and one years of the old-world folk, and some with a new and terrible mortality upon them. As for Bove Derg and all the Fairy Host, the wild thistle waved over their nameless graves. Lir lay beneath the grass outside his great dun of Shee Finnaha. His last words had been : " I hear the beating of wings. O wild swans, I hear the beating of thy wings."

Thereafter Irbir the Harper moved aimlessly away, and with him passed the shadow of the greatness that was gone.

The children of Lir now spoke wearily among themselves of what they should do. At the last they decided to go back to the Isle of Glora, and there await the fulfilment of their doom.

One more night they spent at Shee Finnaha, mourning over the grey sorrow of Lir, and over the desolation of that noble place, and over the ruin of the Dedannan folk. So wild and mournful was their singing that night that the beasts of the forest congregated round the ruined dun, and from the crags of the hills thronged the cliff-hawks and the eagles. In the heart of the woods Irbir, the old harper, died, dreaming that he was in Tir-nan-Og, the Land of Youth, and was listening again to the voices of Love.

On the morrow the children of Lir flew sorrowfully away from Shee Finnaha and returned to Innis Glora. They alit at a small lake in the heart of that isle, and there began once more to sing their slow, sweet, fairy music.

So wonderful was their singing, with all its added pain and the mystery of years, that the birds of all the regions round were wont to collect daily, and gather in flocks round about the singing swans.  Thus it was that the little lake came to be called the Lake of the Bird Flocks.

At sunrise these innumerable birds would disperse far and wide ; some seaward, some inland, some northward to Achill, some as far south as the three rocks known as Donn's Sea-Rest, some to Inniskea—to this day called the Isle of the Lonely Crane, for there dwells, and has dwelled since the beginning of the world, and shall dwell till the day of flame, a solitary brooding crane.  But at night every bird returned to Innis Glora, to hear the slow, sweet, fairy music of the children of Lir.

In this way the years went past.

On a day of the days Fionula called her brothers to listen to her, because of a dream that she had dreamed.

" The Taillkenn[1] has come at last," she said. " I saw a strange light in the East at midnight. A star rose out of it, and travelled through the gulfs of the sky, and rested over Erin, and sank slowly over this our dear land.

---

[1] St. Patrick.  (Druidic name.)

Then I heard a smoke of voices rising to the stars, and thence, too, came a chiming sweeter than any chants we have sung in all these thrice three hundred years."

On the eve of that day a man came forth from the mainland in a coracle. He came to Innis Glora, and alighted there, and kneeled in a strange fashion, and supplicated some god.

It was St. Kemoc.

After nightfall the wild swans were silent, for all were heavy with the strangeness of this man, who was not like unto any Dedannan or even a Milesian, and who prayed on his knees, and supplicated a god set beyond the stars.

In the grey dawn they awoke, trembling. Trembling still, they started and ran bewilderedly to and fro, for strange and dreadful to them was the sound that they heard. It was but a little sound, and faint and afar; but it was the chiming of a bell, and in all the thrice three hundred years and more they had lived they had heard nought like it. The bell was the matin-bell of St. Kemoc, but they knew it not, nor what it meant. Aed and Fiachra and Conn ran wildly and far, but at last when the bell ceased, they returned to Fionula.

"Do you know what this sound is, this faint, fearful sound that has terrified us, dear brothers?"

"No, we have heard the faint, fearful voice, but know not what it is. Is it the voice of the strange man who has come among us, and is he a god?"

"No," answered Fionula, with grave joy, "but it is the voice of the Christians' bell. Soon we shall be free of our spell; soon we shall have peace. It is the bell we have dreamed of for so many years."

All were glad at that. Kemoc had again begun to ring his matin-bell, and the four swans crouched low, listening to its strange music. When it ceased, Fionula spoke:

"Let us now sing our music."

Therewith they sang their slow, sweet, fairy music.

Kemoc rose in his place, amazed with great wonder. At first he thought it was the voices of the angels singing in Paradise. Then suddenly it was revealed to him that it was the slow, sweet, fairy music of the children of Lir, whereat he rejoiced exceedingly, for he had fared westward in the hope to find and save Fionula and Aed and Fiachra and Conn, of whom he had heard soon after he came to Erin with tidings of Christ and the Christian faith.

So when his prayers were done, and sunrise put a shine of gold upon the sea, Kemoc rose and went to the lake, and hailed the four white swans. And when they answered and told him who they were, he gave thanks to God.

"Come now to land," he added, "and sojourn with me, for it is in this place that ye are destined to be freed from your enchantment."

Filled with a great joy on hearing the words of the Christian saint, they came ashore, and went with him to where he had builded his cell against the forefront of a cave.

Three days later a skilled craftsman for whom he had sent came to Innis Glora, and wrought two slender shining chains of silver. These St. Kemoc put upon Fionula and Aed and upon Fiachra and Conn, to show that they were now bondagers to Christ, for all that they were still swans and under the doom of the spell of Aeifa.

Thereafter the time passed with joy and peace. Kemoc taught them the holy faith, and came to love them with his whole heart. As for the children of Lir they were glad with so great a gladness that they remembered no more their long misery, and even loved better to hear the hymns and litanies of St. Kemoc than the lifesweet war-chants and love-songs they had heard in their childhood from Irbir and other bards and minstrels.

But at that time[1] there was a queen in Erin who above all other things desired the glory of having these marvellous singing swans as her own. In the olden days men and women were wont to hold the decrees of the gods and of fate in reverence; and more thought was taken of the inner meanings of dreams, marvels, and the strange vicissitudes of life. Has not a wise poet declared that the smaller the soul the greater the tyranny? This queen was Decca, daughter of Finghin, king of Munster, and wife of Lairgnen, the king of Connaught.

It was of these two that Aeifa, long, long ago, had spoken prophetically, but none remembered this save only Fionula, in whose

---

[1] With the advent of St. Kemoc, the story comes within historical times. Lairgnen and Finghin were kings of Connaught and Munster, who flourished in the seventh century A.D.

mind dreams and memories floated as water-blooms on a mountain lake—the blooms that float and sink and rise as though a breath sustained or swayed them, the breath out of still, pellucid depths.

At last the desire of Decca overmastered her. She begged Lairgnen to fare westward to Kemoc, and obtain the swans from the saint and bring them to her. But this the king feared to do, nor held it a kingly act. Then Decca gave way to her anger, and left the great house of the king and vowed that she would not sleep there another night till Lairgnen brought her the singing swans.

So the woman fled southward into Munster, her father's realm.

Lairgnen the Connaught king loved his wife to weakness. He was the slave of her dark eyes and her smiling lips and her selfish heart and her poor will: so he came to evil then, and later. For according as a man's love is, and as he loves to strength, so shall his life be abased or uplifted.

So Lairgnen sent messengers after Decca, and sought her in the south. Thus was the prophecy fulfilled.

The woman returned, but put a bond upon

the king.  He was weak, and she made a sport of him as women do who are loved to weakness and not to strength : as with men also, when women love them ignobly, and not as high mate with high mate.

Thus it came about that Lairgnen gave the word to St. Kemoc that he desired the four swans to be sent to him at his royal house in Connaught.  Kemoc, however, refused.  He served the King of kings, not the king of Connaught.

Full of wrath, Lairgnen set out for the western coast, and at last reached Innis Glora.  When he asked Kemoc if he had indeed refused to give up the swans at his command, and was told that this was so, he swore the old pagan oath by the sun and the moon and the wind, and vowed that he would not leave that place without them.

"Doom must be fulfilled, O king," said Kemoc, "but woe unto that man by whom the evil of a day of the days is wrought."

Lairgnen laughed, and followed the saint into the little chapel where the four swans stood before the altar, singing a sweet wonderful song that was a hymn of peace and joy.  Seizing the silver chain of Fionula and Aed in one hand, and that of Fiachra and Conn in the other, he forced them to follow him.

"Do not do this thing, Lairgnen, son of Colman," said St. Kemoc.

"And for why not?" asked the king, smiling grimly, as he neared the door of the wattle-church. "Am I not the king, and can I not do as I will in mine own lands?"

"There is another King. If thou doest a wrong against Him, thou shalt have neither the desire of thine heart nor yet go free of the penalty of lifelong sorrow and a bitter end."

For a moment Lairgnen quailed. The angry voice of a cleric was a perilous omen in those days. Then he strode forward, dragging after him the four swans.

Suddenly a wild, strange cry resounded over the church. All stood silent, appalled. To Fionula only was it revealed that it was neither the screaming of the wind, nor the thin shrewd wail of the sea, nor the savage cry of a sea-mew —but that it was the voice of Aeifa, that lost forlorn demon of the air for whom there might be no rest now till the day of the flame of which St. Kemoc spoke.

"Come!" said Lairgnen, with a great effort.

But when he strove with the chains, lo! a strange thing happened. These fell apart, and at the same moment the great wings of the swans contracted, and the white feathers that were the beauty of their bodies shrivelled. A mist of blown feathers was about them: and when Lairgnen and Kemoc looked through this as it settled upon the ground like dust, they beheld a wonderful and a terrible thing.

For as the feathers fell away from the children of Lir, Fionula and her brothers once more regained their human shape. But now they were no longer fair and sweet and young, as they were when Aeifa put her enchantment upon them. They stood there, worn with intolerable age. Grey and ashy were their bodies, and long and sere and white their thin, blanched hair: and they were tremulous as reeds, and their wan hands were as the shaking wan leaves of the poplar when autumn is dead.

The children of Lir looked one upon the other with dim, forlorn eyes. It was a bitter thing to live so many ages only to find that their own kith and kin were as dust, and that their habitation was a wilderness, and that their very race had passed away: to see each other in human form again, but Fionula an aged ancient woman, grey as old hanging moss and wrinkled as the wave-rippled sand, and tall Aed and swift Fiachra and laughing Conn as three feeble old men, wavering as their own shadows.

When Lairgnen saw this he was overcome with dread. He uttered a strange cry, and, averting his face, fled from the little chapel, nor looked back once upon Innis Glora; and feared the following flight of his own shadow till once more he reached his great house in Connaught, over which he heard a demon of the air wailing and laughing, and knew that it was Aeifa, and that the terror of this banshee would be with him and his for ever.

As he fled, he heard the bitter execrations of St. Kemoc, but these he heeded less than the thin, inarticulate murmur of the voices of the children of Lir, like the hum of gnats in a well.

Nevertheless Kemoc himself was able to hear the whisper of Fionula. So one may hear the faint rustle of leaves in the heart of a forest where there is no wind.

" Be swift, holy one, and give us baptism, here before the altar. We have but a brief while wherein to draw breath. Great is thy sorrow at this parting, but not more great than is ours. Nevertheless the end is always in the beginning, and we are but the dry thistledown of the young sprays of green. For thee, too, O Kemoc, the vial of silence shall be broken, but not until thy hair is like the foam of the sea, and thine eyes dim as the light beneath a wave."

Thereupon St. Kemoc led them slowly towards the altar, and bade farewell to each, for he saw that the shadow of death had covered them from the soles of the feet to the chin of the head, and was rising to the eyes.

Once more Fionula spoke.

"Farewell, dear brothers," she said. "We are so old that we have forgotten age. Very weary should we be were it not for sweet death. We go far hence, and it may well be that we visit Hy Brásil before we see the shining of the gates of Paradise. There we shall greet our father Lir, and he shall come with us. And if he come not, we shall abide with him, for love is stronger than death."

"Even so," whispered Aed and Fiachra and Conn.

"And to thee, Kemoc, thou holy one," she

murmured, "I have this thing for the saying. We are of our people, and would fain be in the darkness as our ancient forgotten dead before us. It is not fitting that we lie in the earth who are of the old race, and have the blood of kings, and have lived in no dishonour, and die as we have lived."

"Speak, Fionula."

"When we fail utterly and perish, as we shall do within this hour that is upon us, O Kemoc, remember that as in life I so often sheltered my brothers against my breast and sides when we were swans, we must not be apart in death. Therefore bury us on this spot and in one grave.[1] And in that grave let Conn stand near me at my right side, and Fiachra at my left, and let Aed my twin-brother be before my face."

With that she sighed. So sighs a wan, drifting leaf wind-slidden over sere grass.

Then Kemoc baptized Fionula and Aed and Fiachra and Conn: and when he had given them eternity and the company of saints, they died. They did not fall, but wavered as dry

---

[1] It was the wont among the early Celtic peoples to bury their dead erect, particularly in the case of kings, and great warriors, and sons and daughters of kings.

reeds, and were suddenly at one with their own shadows, and were no more.

When the saint rose from his knees, he put the tears from his face and stared into the deeps of heaven. Then he had the joy of a glad vision. Overhead he beheld four children with light silver-shining wings, their faces radiant : yet knew not whether they were little ones or were youthful with new life, for the glory dazzled him. A moment, as the foam-bells on a falling wave, they were there : then they vanished, and passed westward, and were in Hy Brásil with Lir and their own people even while Kemoc bent lamenting over the frail ancient bodies that had been the children of Lir.

So in that place a grave was digged, and Fionula was placed standing therein : and by her right side, Conn ; and by her left, Fiachra ; and before her face, Aed. Over this grave Kemoc raised a mound, and put a great stone upon it. Then he made a lament over the dead.

When all the people were gone, there remained only Kemoc, and a young poet and cleric named Ebric the son of Ebric, the son of Ebric of Irros Domnann. And when St.

Kemoc went to his cell, and knew the dark hour, because of his sorrow, Ebric stood by the great stone at the mound and graved in Ogham the names of Fionula and Aed and Fiachra and Conn.

The salt grasses wave out of the dust, the dust of the powder of that stone which Ebric graved with cunning hand : but out of the hearts of men who shall take the sorrowful tale of the Children of Lir, or against it shall prevail what frost of age, what breath of time ?

The stone perisheth, but the winged word on the breath of the lips endureth for ever.

# The Fate of
the Sons of Turenn

Turenn interceding for his sons.

To face p. 117.]

# The Fate of
# the Sons of Turenn

I WILL tell you now the old heroic saga of the Fate of the Sons of Turenn : how they paid the great eric laid upon them by Lu the Long-Handed, called the Ildanna because of his great wisdom in all magic craft and Dedannan lore ; and how at the last their dauntless bravery was as sand before the wind, as mist before the sun, as dew upon the grass.

It is one of the most ancient of tales. Brian, Ur, and Urba, the sons of Turenn, did their great wrong upon Kian, the father of Lu of the Long Hand, and paid their unheard-of and heroic eric, when Bove Derg, the last king of the Dedannans, was still a youth—and that was long before the Children of Lir were changed into four white swans.

No Milesian had been seen in Erin in those

days. Nevertheless the power of the Dedannans was already broken, though they were still foremost in green Banba, as the bards loved to call Erin, after a great queen who had reigned there, when the Fairy Host was supreme: for the fierce Fomorian pirates of the north had descended upon them again and again like a devastating plague, and at last their High King, the King of Lochlin, Balor of the Evil Eye, had subdued them into bondage.

Year by year, and that for the fourth part of a year, Balor sent his emissaries to collect tribute. The men were of the greatest and fiercest of the black Fomorians, so called because they were black-haired and black-bearded, with fells as coarse and thick as those of wild boars. These men were dreaded by the Dedannans, for they appeared to be beyond all reach of magic spells, and to have more terrible arms and an invincible power in warfare.

At that time Nuadh of the Silver Hand was High King of Erin. He was the most prudent of all the Dedannan kings, but there were many of the wisest druids and bards even in his own day who lamented that he was over-prudent, and that it would be wiser to risk all in order to regain honour and freedom than to lose all for the sake of an inglorious peace. Nevertheless, so great was the love of life among the people at large, and so keen was their desire to be left at peace by the Fomorians, that Nuadh of the Silver Hand put aside his kinglihood, and agreed to pay both tribute and homage.

The yearly tax laid by Balor of the Evil Eye upon Nuadh of the Silver Hand and all the Dedannan folk, was this: a tax separately upon querns, kneading-troughs, and baking-flags, the three things which every Dedannan had to use. Besides this, there was a tax of one gold ounce for every man and woman of the Tuatha-De-Danann. Every year the people had to assemble at the Hill of Tara, where the High King had his palace, and there submit their tribute with many obeisances to the dark, scowling emissaries of Balor of the Evil Eye.

In one year of the years this happened as before. But after Nuadh of the Silver Hand and all his nobles and druids and all the Dedannans had made humble obeisance before the Fomorians, and while the tribute was

being put together, a strange sight was descried.

Coming from the east was a company of
lordly men, splendidly arrayed in white with
gleaming helmets and shields, and riding tall
white horses.  These were headed by a youthful champion of so great a stature and so
warlike a mien, that all men knew he could be
none other than Lu the Long-Handed, son
of Kian the Noble.  All the northlands and
eastlands of Erin were aware of the rumour of
his great valour and worth, and there was at
that day no champion so feared between the
two seas.

Lu, son of Kian, was also of the Dedannans, but he was of the older and rarer
branch, and he and his claimed that the Fairy
Host, of which they formed the chief ornament,
rose or fell by their support.  Among the
splendid company were the sons of Manannan,
son of Lir, the lord of the sea, and other
chieftains and brave knights. Yet, as they
approached, it was Lu of the Long Hand
who held all eyes.  Upon his head was a
golden helmet, wherefrom gleamed two great
shining stones—the eyes of strange gods they
seemed to the people.  His body was covered

with shining armour that was no other than the famous coat of armour of Manannan, through which no weapon might pierce ; and by his side hung the terrible sword, the " Answerer," which had but one answer for every one against whom it was raised—death. The horse, too, that Lu rode was the far-famed stallion of Manannan, so swift that the March wind could not overtake him, nor could water, air, or land offer any obstacles to his progress.

A great shout welcomed these champions of the Fairy Host as they drew near, but this shout came from the assemblage outside of Tara ; and neither the king nor his lords rose at their approach. The Fomorians scowled and stood apart, and then scornfully resumed their tax-gathering.

When they had finished their task the Fomorians rose and together approached the place where the king sat high among his people.

As they drew near, `Nuadh of the Silver Hand and all his lords rose and made humble obeisance.

At this, Lu the Ildanna frowned, and when Lu of the Long Hand frowned his company knew that evil was like to come.

" Tell me, O King," he said haughtily : " why

do you make obeisance to these rude, ungainly folk, and did none to us when we approached, to us who are of the old Dedannan race?"

Thereupon Nuadh of the Silver Hand spake the bitterness of truth, and how it was that in order to save the land from devastation, and his people from rapine and outrage, he submitted to the Fomorian yoke. And for the same reason he had not ventured to pay homage to Lu and the Fairy Host, for the Fomorians would have taken this as an insult to Balor of the Evil Eye, and some great evil would have ensued.

Lu smiled scornfully.

"And at the worst, O Nuadh of the Silver Hand, there is a disastrous end and death. What then? Is not death the sure end of all men, and is not disaster the lot of many a hero as well as of many a slave?"

"That is so, Ildanna."

"Then why evade that shadow, and all because of fear of these dark pirates out of the north. Is not honour better than safety, and is not shame a worse death than to be slain?"

"Even so, Ildanna. Nevertheless, I wish to avoid vain bloodshed. There can be but one end. Why should I ruin my people?"

"Ruin is not a sure thing, O King : but if it were, better ruin than dishonour."

"Dost thou speak as a lord of high birth, or as one of the common people?"

"I speak as the son of Kian the Noble."

"Even so ; but for each noble in my kingdom there are a thousand Dedannans of no rank.  I am their king.  I speak for them."

For a time thereafter Lu sat brooding. His silence was worse than his scornful words. Nuadh the King saw what was in his mind, and dreaded that he would go forth in his wrath.  Thrice he half rose as though to lay hands upon Lu to restrain him, and thrice he sat back uncertain what to do.

Then suddenly Lu rose, and in the eyes of all men drew slowly from its sheath his great white sword.  At sight of the "Answerer," there was a shiver among the Dedannans, so great was the terrible fame of this sword, but still more because the drawing of it there and then by Lu of the Long Hand meant that the flame was in his blood.

"Beware!" cried the king.

But Lu laughed a grim laugh.  Then, lifting the "Answerer" on high, and knitting his brows into a heavy frown, he sprang in among the Fomorians.

It was like the leap of lightning among wild cattle, that. Hither and thither the "Answerer" flashed, and at each blow a Fomorian head whirled to the ground ; yea, as a sharp prow will divide the wave-crest from the wave, so the great sword severed the head from the shoulders of each Fomorian, shoring through helmet or thick fell of hair as through water.

It was not till a whirlwind of swords flashed and circled around Lu that those about him woke from their stupor. Then with a loud shout the sons of Manannan and others of the Fairy Host leaped forward and joined in the fray.

The Fomorians fought with fury, being wrought to madness by the thought that they were as chaff before these newcomers, in the face of the whole Dedannan nation—for so great was their scorn of the people they held in bondage that death at their hands seemed doubly accursed.

But before Lu of the Long Hand and his Fairy Host there was no withstaying. By tens and scores the Fomorians fell, as swaying grain before the reaper. Everywhere, flashing like a meteor, the white gleam of the Answerer rose and fell, the pulse of death.

At last only nine of the Fomorian pirates survived, and these clustered upon a low rising, and fought desperately to the end.  Suddenly the tides of battle ceased, and this was because of the voice of Lu Ildanna.

He looked scornfully at the remnant of the proud Fomorians.  These were now sullenly at bay, foreseeing death only, and not un-willingly now that the despised Dedannans had brought them to so sore a pass.

" Let these dogs go ! " exclaimed Lu.

At the bitter words, the emissaries of King Balor of Lochlin gripped their swords anew, and ground their teeth in impotent rage. More they could not do, for even in their brief breathing space they saw that they were beset by a hedge of spears.

" Let these dogs go ! " Lu said again. Then, addressing them, he added :

" Look ye, ye carrion wolves, we spare your lives only that ye may fare back to your dens in the north, and tell that unkingly king, Balor of the Evil Eye, that which we have done unto your company.  And say this also, that if he come hither, we shall do unto him and his, that which we have done unto these dead men who were once your fellows." With that the nine Fomorians departed, scowling fiercely and below their breath muttering imprecations and menaces.

That night the beacons of joy flared out across valley and plain, from the hill of Tara, and great were the rejoicings throughout the land. Only Nuadh of the Silver Hand dreamed uneasily for that and many other nights ; knowing well that Balor of the Evil Eye would not let pass the slight which had been put upon him. And after all, it was but a handful of the Fomorian host which had been slain on the Plains of Tara. Nevertheless, the king hoped that he might be spared the wrath of Balor, for none of the Dedannans whom he ruled had taken part in the fray, but only those who were of the company of Lu of the Long Hand.

Bitter, indeed, was the wrath of Balor, when he heard what had been done to his Fomorian emissaries.

" The Dedannans shall soon be but a memory," he exclaimed ; " their kings and nobles shall utterly perish, and of all their race none shall survive save those who shall

be slaves for ever to my people.  Their very
land, that green Eri they are so fain of, shall
be no more than an unregarded province of
Lochlin."

Thereafter, Balor sent word throughout all
Lochlin, from the Cape of the Midnight Sun
to the Narrow Seas,[1] and bade all the peoples
who owned him king to assemble speedily for
war; and in every haven he bade the sea-
galleys to be got ready.

This took many weeks, and thereafter was
the slow waiting for the coming of spring.
But at last all was ready, and then Bras, the
son of Balor, led forth the mightiest host which
had ever sailed from the shores of Lochlin.

This vast concourse of galleys sailed northward before favouring winds, and then westward along the storm-swept coasts of Alba, and
at last southward again by the Hebrid Isles.
Thence, with fresh provisions and replenished
water-barrels, they sailed towards and round
the northern headlands of Eri, and like a great
flock of sea-vultures settled upon the coasts of
Connaught.

With laughter and fierce disdain the Fomori-

---

[1] *i.e.*, from the north of Norway to the coasts of Denmark.

ans spread far and wide, and at once began to despoil the country, and lay waste the tilled lands. In the ears of all rang the arrogant parting words of Balor of the Evil Eye: "And when at the last ye have cut off for me the head of that man Lu, called the Ildanna, then put a mighty cable around this troublesome Isle of Erin, and tow it back with your ships, and lay it alongside the north coasts of our Lochlin."

But meanwhile all the realms of the Tuatha-De-Danann were smitten with fear. None dared await the dreaded Fomorians, and everywhere were flying hordes of men and women and children, chariots, horses, and cattle.

The king of Connaught in that day was Bove Derg, son of the Dagda, he who afterwards became the last Dedannan king. Straightway he sent word to Lu Ildanna, begging him to raise a host and succour the men of Connaught, as otherwise not a man would be left to stay the advance of the Fomorians.

Lu of the Long Hand was sorrowful that by his action he had brought this curse upon the lands of Erin, yet he knew that it was better than the old shame. By the Sun and

Moon and Wind he swore that he would do all he could to raise a host, and himself give battle to Bras and his Fomorians.

With all speed he hasted to Dunree, and was glad indeed when he saw the Hill of Tara rise from the plain. For of a surety he held that Nuadh of the Silver Hand would join with the princes of Erin and fight the invader.

That surety was in vain. Nuadh refused to go into battle.

" When Bras leads his Fomorians towards the Hill of Tara," he said, " that will be time for me to raise the banner against him."

" Listen, Nuadh of the Silver Hand, art thou not High King?" exclaimed Lu.

" Even so, Ildanna."

" And is not thy first duty to lead the princes of Erin against the invader? If we are all as one, we can laugh at Balor of the Evil Eye and all the host he sends against us. If we are divided we shall surely fall."

But for all the pleadings of Lu Ildanna, Nuadh refused to take the field. He had one answer to all pleas.

" Bras and his Fomorian host do no more than lay waste the lands of Connaught. Let then the king of Connaught see to his own.

I have sent friendly messages to Balor, and in order to keep the peace have offered alliance and even to pay tribute again. But till war is declared against me I will do nothing."

Furious against Nuadh of the Silver Hand, Lu Ildanna rode away.

"Dust upon thy home," he muttered, "were it not for the ruin upon all Erin. Nevertheless, I have but one thing to do."

Lu had not ridden far, when his heart rejoiced because of three strong warriors he saw approaching.

These were his father, Kian, and the two brothers of his father, Ald and Art. In that day the seven fairest champions in the northlands of Erin were Lu himself, Kian and his two brothers, and Brian, Ur, and Urba, the sons of Turenn. Each of these was a host in himself, both because of his own valour and for the great influence that each had upon the clansmen of the north.

In a brief while Lu told all, and begged the aid of these three chiefs for Bove Derg, and not for Bove Derg only, but for the honour and safety of Erin.

Kian and Ald and Art were wroth with the high king.

"The first duty of a king is kinglihood," said Kian.

"And without deathless courage a king is dead," said Ald.

"And without sleepless eyes a king is a sluggard," said Art.

"A king should be to all men what each man would fain be to himself," said Lu. "My father Kian says well: the first duty of a king is kinglihood. But since Nuadh of the Silver Hand is fain to rest at ease in his dun, under the safe shadow of Tara, so let him rest. We are men, and must act."

Therewith all took counsel, and while Lu rode westward, to raise all whom he could to succour the men of Connaught, Ald and Art rode southward.

"I shall go north," said Kian.

"Why so?" asked Lu, knowing that it would be best for his father to go eastward.

"The wind bloweth that way," answered Kian lightly. But truly enough none knew that in that answer and in that riding northward, was the beginning of the long and dreadful tragedy of which, for generations thereafter, the bards sang as The Fate of the Sons of Turenn.

*　　　*　　　*　　　*

At this point Peterkin rose from where he kneeled beside Eilidh, and went over to Ian Mor and took his hand and looked long at him.

"These words I have heard you say again and again, Ian—*Ma tha sin an Dan*, if it be Destiny—what do they mean?"

"I cannot tell you, Peterkin; for to me they mean everything."

"But must Kian come to sorrow because he followed the way of the wind?"

"I cannot tell you, Peterkin. But of this you may be sure, that no man needs to do this or that thing because of the way of the wind or anything else. Only, behind all doings of men there is a wind that blows. That is the wind of Destiny. That is what I meant when I said that Kian, choosing lightly to go the way of the wind, and by his own choice, yet went the way of Fate."

"And is Fate a man?"

"No."

"Have you ever seen it?"

"No."

"Has any one ever seen it?"

"No."

Peterkin laughed below his breath.

" Ivor Maclean, the boatman, told me that 'an Dan' was only a shadow before and behind, and that none need trouble about a shadow."

" And what do *you* think, Peterkin ?"

"I think that 'an Dan' is only a shadow before and behind; and I laugh to see my shadow, but I do not fear it. It is only a shadow."

" Peterkin is right, Ian," said Eilidh, in a low voice. "And do you remember what was said long ago about wisdom coming out of the mouths of little children ?"

"Yes," Ian answered slowly and gravely, " Peterkin is right."

But Peterkin only laughed merrily, as suddenly he sprang up.

"See," he exclaimed, "my shadow has leapt from beside me, till now it is fading along the wall. When I laughed it leapt away."

Well, resumed Ian Mor, Kian was not many miles forth upon the great pastures to the north of Tara, when he saw three lordly men riding towards him.

They were still a great way off, but Kian

the Noble was noted far and wide for his keen sight, and he knew who the mailed and shining ones were. They were Dedannans, but they were of a clan at bitter feud with his own ; and his heart quailed as he saw that in that lonely place he would have to meet face to face with Brian, Ur, and Urba, the sons of Turenn. Far better would it have been for him to ride forward fearlessly, and call upon the sons of Turenn to put all enmity aside in the face of the bitter danger to Erin because of Bras and his Fomorians. But a man born under a dark star must soon or late ride into the shadow of that star.

So when Kian had realized that the foes of him and his house were fast approaching, he cast about for some way to delude the sons of Turenn. Already they had seen the stranger, though they had not recognised him.

In common with all the lords of the Dedannans, Kian carried with him a magic wand. With this he could at any time transform himself into some living creature. And so it happened that, while he was still pondering, he caught sight of a vast herd of swine feeding upon the thistle-pastures to the left ; and no sooner had he done so than he took his

wand and changed himself into a boar.  His
horse, too, he changed; and then both, graz-
ing often, joined the great herd, and were soon
at one with it.

Kian laughed to himself at how he had
outwitted the sons of Turenn, but oversoon
did he laugh.  After all he was sorrowful; for
it was not seemly for a man to change himself
into a pig, lest death or some disaster came
upon him in that guise: for, according as a
man's doom came to him, so would he have to
bear it.

Meanwhile the three sons of Turenn rode
across the plain.  Fair to see were they,
these three comely lords: Brian, the eldest
and strongest; Ur, the tallest and fairest; and
Urba the swift.  They had seen Kian riding
slowly towards them, but had not thought
more than that he was an emissary from
Dunree, where Nuadh of the Silver Hand was.
When, however, they missed him suddenly,
Brian frowned and drew rein.

"Tell me, my brothers," he exclaimed,
"where is he whom a brief while ago we saw
riding toward us?"

"He is no longer to be seen," Urba answered.  "Yet there is no hiding-place that

we wot of. If he were lying on the grass, we should descry him and his horse from where we now are."

"They are not on the grass," said Ur; "for I could see a slim greyhound were it lying there."

Brian pondered awhile. Then he spoke again.

"As ye know well, war is all about us now, and it befits us to be wary. It is clear that the man we saw was no friend to us, or why has he hidden himself? But I think I know his secret: with a magic wand he has turned himself into a pig, and is now among that great herd of swine that we see yonder."

"Then he has escaped us, Brian?"

"Not so, Ur. I too have my magic wand with me; with it I shall now turn my two brothers into swift hounds. Ye shall then speed in among these swine and see if ye can root out this man, who is surely an enemy."

And with that Brian took his wand, and changed his brothers into hounds; and they raced away with the speed of the wind, while he rode swiftly towards a belt of forest which skirted the plain to the rear of the herd.

When the baying of the hounds was heard,

a panic seized upon the swine. Like a great swaying mass of seaweed in the trough of the waves, the herd swung to and fro ; ever becoming more and more densely packed, and squealing and grunting in terror and bewilderment as the two gaunt hounds sprang against their heaving masses or dashed to and fro in their midst.

At the east they were so driven in upon themselves, that they became as one solid mass, close-wedged. Among these dense hundreds it seemed impossible for Ur and Urba to find the enchanted man ; but while they were still running to and fro in their eager quest, Brian saw a pig leap from the rear of the herd and run swiftly towards the belt of forest.

Brian put his horse upon the wind, as the saying is ; and it was a race then between the mounted man and the enchanted boar : but just as the first undergrowth was nigh Brian came up with the fleeing animal, and drove his hunting-spear in betwixt its shoulders.

With a terrible scream the flying boar rolled over ; then, with a wild human crying and speech, begged for pity.

"Oh, son of Turenn," it cried, "have pity

upon me! Sure it is an evil deed to slay me thus, well knowing who I am!"

"I know that thy voice is the voice of a man," answered Brian, "but I know not who thou art. I am Brian, eldest of the sons of Turenn. Tell me thy name."

"He who implores thy mercy, O Brian of the Oak Shaft, is Kian, the father of thy comrade in years and arms, Lu of the Long Hand."

By this time Ur and Urba were beside the victor and the victim, and now resumed their human shape. When they heard the pleadings of Kian they interceded for him, notwithstanding the deadly feud between the clans of Turenn and Kian. But Brian would not listen to their counsel, not even when Ur pleaded that great evil might come out of the slaying of Kian, nor when Urba urged that this was not the day and the hour for such a deed, when Erin needed every man to fight against the Fomorians. And, of a truth, that has ever been the sad way of the Gael, who will think of the private wrong first, than of the general weal, and so will fall as a single tree will fall where a forest would be steadfast.

When Kian saw that his fate was come upon him, and heard Brian swear by a sacred oath that he would not spare him though he returned thrice to life, or seven times changed his form, he made one last supplication.

"At the least, as ye are honourable men, save me this dishonour.  Let me not die as a pig, but as a man.  I have dropped my magic wand; therefore, O Brian, I pray of thee to take thine, and with it restore me to mine own form."

"That shall be done," said the chief, adding scornfully, "for sure it is an easier thing for me to kill a man than a pig."

But no sooner was Kian a man again than he laughed mockingly.

"Why do you laugh thus?" asked Ur.

"I laugh because I have outwitted ye at the last, ye sons of Turenn.  What is death to me who have a dust of grey hairs over my once black locks, or is death indeed a thing at any time to fear overmuch?  Ill as it would befit me to die as a pig, still more ill would it be because of that which follows death."

"Speak," said Ur, though in his heart both he and his brothers knew what Kian was about to say.

"I have outwitted ye, as I have said; for if as a pig I had been slain by Brian of the Oak Shaft, then ye would have had no other eric to pay for me than the eric of a pig, but now ye shall have to pay the eric of a man, and upon that the eric of a father of grown sons, and upon that the fatherhood eric of each son, and upon that the eric of a great lord, and upon that the eric of the broken honour of my son Lu of the Long Hand. And I tell ye this, that never has there been, nor ever will be, so great an eric as that which ye shall have to pay for this deed of thine, so that in the years to come men shall speak of the eric of the sons of Turenn as the most difficult and the worst that was ever paid in Erin."

"That may be," said Brian sullenly, "but we shall slay thee here, in this waste place, and none shall know when death came to thee, or where thou liest, and for all that thy son Lu is Lu the Ildanna, he shall seek in vain to know where the worms make merry upon thee."

"In the shadow of death I see clearly, and I see that death will not put his silence upon me till Lu has learned the evil deed that has been done."

"Spare him," urged Urba, "for of a surety he is already sore wounded, and he did no more than seek to escape us. It would be well, Brian, not to have this man's blood upon us."

"Spare him," pleaded Ur, "for innocent blood is an ill thing to spill. This man did not come upon us with lifted spear or sword, but, seeing that we were three and he one only, sought to escape. It is not a knightly deed to take the life of a stricken man, and of one who asks for mercy."

"We will slay him," said Brian sullenly.

"Remember this," pleaded Ur, "that if we slay him, Urba and I must pay the penalty along with thee, and that it is a hard thing upon us who would fain spare this man."

Brian laughed.

"If ye and Urba fear the eric, ye may go hence at once. I will do my own slaying. But ye forget that the sons of Turenn are under *geas* to have no quarrel that is not the quarrel of each, and to fight no fight wherein each doth not front it in the same hour and place."

"We do not forget," answered Ur and Urba; and each added: "Do as thou wilt, Brian, our elder brother."

So Brian turned to where Kian lay upon the stony thistle-strewn grass.

"Hast thou aught more to say?"

"This only, that no eric ever paid shall be counted as near unto that which ye shall have to pay, and that the weapons wherewith ye slay me shall cry out to Lu my son, and tell him what ye three have done unto me."

Again Brian laughed.

"Thou who fled before us as a pig shalt die as a trapped beast. We shall not give thee the honour of death by the clean sword or the deft spear."

With that he stooped and raised on high a huge angular slab of stone, grey below, and mossed and lichened above, and, swaying with the weight, hurled it down upon the head of Kian. Then Ur and Urba lifted other great stones, and did likewise, because of their bond. And this was how death came to Kian the Noble.

When the old chief lay still and white at last, the three sons of Turenn made haste to hide his body from sight; so they dug a great hole in the sandy grass, and buried the slain man.

There was a strange trembling in the earth

that day, a trembling felt throughout Erin from sea to sea, and men marvelled and feared.

But none so much marvelled as Brian and Ur and Urba, for when they had buried the bruised body of Kian they saw with horror that the shaking earth threw it back again. Nevertheless, once more they buried it, and deeper, and put heavy stones upon the trodden sods. Then, to their still greater horror and amaze, the earth again trembled and again threw back the murdered dead.

At that Ur and Urba wished to ride away at once from the accursed place, but Brian would not.

"Fate is made by men, as well as that Fate rules men," he said. "I shall not rest content till the earth holds at last the body of Kian, son of Kian the White."

Yet it was not until the seventh time that the earth trembled no more, and held within it, beneath a cairn of boulders, the slain body of Kian the Noble.

Thereafter the three sons of Turenn rode swiftly away, and that night were among the host which had been assembled by Lu of the Long Hand.

On the morrow, on the vast plains of

Moytura, the great and terrible Battle of the Kites was fought. It was so called because after a day of dreadful slaughter the kites and hawks assembled in multitudes, and were satiated with the feast of the dead. In that battle the fiercest strife was on the part of four heroes : Lu the Ildanna, and the three sons of Turenn. For hours the swaying and whirling of spears, the rush of javelins, the flashing of swords, the trampling of horses and crash of war-chariots, made the plain of Moytura a place of savage din and fury. For long it seemed as though the great might and numbers of the Fomorians would give the day to Bras, son of Balor of the Evil Eye ; but so great was the prowess of the Dedannan host, that the Fomorians were mowed down as ripe grain.

In the wane of the afternoon, Bras and Lu met at last. The tides of war ceased, for all men wished to see the battle-meeting of these two champions.

But already Bras had seen that the day had gone against the glory of Lochlin, and he knew that an hour hence his great army would be utterly routed, and that all who did not straightway escape to the shores of Connaught and gain the Fomorian galleys would be tracked and cut down like flying wolves.

So he lowered his great spear, and threw his shield upon the ground, and thereafter asked Lu to stay the tides of battle, and agreed that the day should be accounted as a final victory to the men of Erin. And the son of the king of Lochlin further agreed, that if Lu and the leaders of the Dedannans would do this, he would give a solemn bond to withdraw all the Fomorians from Erin, to cancel for ever the bond put upon the Tuatha-De-Danann by Balor of the Evil Eye, and never to return again in enmity, neither he nor any Fomorian of the north nor southlander of lower Lochlin.

And thus it was that the great battle of Moytura, the Battle of the Kites, came to an end. A year thereafter the grass was not yet green, and the plain was covered with the white bones of the innumerous dead.

When all was over, and Bras and his defeated army were hasting towards the distant Connaught shores, Lu threw from him his blood-stained armour and the weapons he was almost too weary to bear. All day he had fought, as only the mightiest heroes fight, and many strong and valorous men had marvelled at his dauntless courage and at the prowess that failed not for one moment.

Glad was Lu of the Long Hand to see Ald and Art, but when he asked how his father had fared in the battle, and heard that he had not been there, and had been seen of no man that day, he knew that Kian the Noble was no longer alive.

"For," he said, "if my father were alive he would have been with me this day, or, if peradventure that were not possible, would have sent me a sign. Howsoever this may be, something within me tells that my father is no longer among the living. And now, ye who hear me, listen, for by the Sun and the Moon and the Wind I swear that I shall not slake this bitter thirst of mine, nor rest this over-weary head, until I have found how and where and when an evil fate came upon my father, whom I loved as I have loved and love none other."

That night Lu Ildanna, with a hundred chosen men, rode swiftly to Tara, but there found no word of Kian.

On the morrow he set forth at dawn, alone; for in a dream it had come to him that his father lay moaning beneath the thistle-strewn grass on the stony plain of Moy Murhenna. And there, in truth, Lu came upon the end of his quest; for as he rode slowly and sadly across the plain, whereon he could not discern a living being save a vast herd of swine, he heard, as one may hear in a shell, a plaintive sighing.

"What is that sighing?" he cried. "Is it the death-sigh of thee, Kian my father?"

There was no answer save the strange sighing, that was not of the wind or any moving thing, but seemed now to come from above, now from around, now from beneath. But at the third asking, a voice answered, thin and feeble:

"It is the death-sighing of me, Kian thy father, O Lu my son."

"And who put death upon thee, thou who liest there in the darkness of the shadow of death?"

"The three sons of Turenn slew me here in this waste place. And because that they slew me in no fair strife, and because that they finished their slaying by crushing me with great stones till there was not left of me one bone alive, I cry to thee, O Lu my son, whom men now call Lu the Ildanna, because of thy craft and wisdom, to see that a greater eric be exacted for me than has ever yet been exacted in Erin for any slain man. And in the end see that thou sparest not, for otherwise there shall be a greater bloodshed still; and ill it befits us, who are noble, that we should bring a tide of blood over Erin, for no worthier cause than the wiping out of that which lies between the clan of Kian and the clan of Turenn."

"As thou sayest, O Kian my father, so shall it be, and even unto the end. And this I swear by the Sun and by the Moon and by the Wind."

Nevertheless, Lu showed no grief till he saw his father's bruised body before him, and then he bewailed bitterly that he had not been nigh when the sons of Turenn drove Kian the Noble to his fate; and bitterly he lamented that one of the noble Dedannan race should be slain by Dedannans; and bitterly he swore that an eric should be exacted such as never before had been heard of in Erin, and that in the end, even were it fulfilled, he should not spare, because of what Kian had foreseen.

At noon Lu returned from Tara, whither

he had gone after he had viewed the speechless dead body of his father, with ten chosen men whom he had bound to silence.

So once more Kian the Noble was placed in his grave, but now standing, as befits a hero. And above the grave they raised a cairn, and midway in this cairn was a great slab of smooth stone, whereon Lu Ildanna graved in Ogam the name and ancestry and great fame of Kian, son of Kian, son of Kian the Thunder-Smith.

But when that night Lu entered Tara again, the whole of the king's town was lit with torches, and resounded with joyous shouts and cries because of the great victory of the Dedannans over the Fomorians; nor was any name so often named as that of Lu Lamfada, Lu the Long-Handed.

When Lu entered the palace of the king, he was received with a mighty shout of welcome, and Nuadh of the Silver Hand himself came to greet him, with fair loving words of praise and gratitude. Right glad was the king to see Lu come to him thus, for he had feared that the Ildanna bore him a bitter grudge because of his having refused his aid to drive forth Bras and his Fomorians.

Therefore it was that he paid honour to Lu Ildanna above all other men, and led him to a seat at his right hand, placing him above the whole assemblage of princes and great lords.

But Lu neither smiled nor made any sign of pleasure. His eyes wandered round the concourse of the Dedannan chivalry. Suddenly his gaze became intent and fixed, for upon three golden-studded seats of honour he beheld the three sons of Turenn.

The high king of Erin was about to speak to his chiefs on the great matter of rejoicing and counsel which had brought them all together, when Lu arose. All stared in amaze, for only some unforeseen emergency could justify a noble speaking before the high king had said what he had to say.

"O King of Erin," said Lu slowly, and in a low voice, yet so clear and cold and vibrant that it was heard of every man in that vast concourse : "O King of Erin, order the chain of silence to be brought hither, and let its soft, delicate music be shaken from it, for I have that to say that must be heard of all men, and not in their ears only but in their hearts and in their minds."

Therewith the Chain of Silence was brought, and was shaken slowly and delicately by the young druid whose charge it was. The sweet low sound rose into the air like fragrance, and passed through all the halls in Tara, and filled the ears of every man, and the mind of each, and the soul of each. There was not a sound in all that place, not a whisper, not a sigh.

In that great silence Lu moved forward till he stood beside the king and faced the whole assemblage.

"Chiefs and warriors of the Tuatha-De-Danann, I have that to ask ye to which I need an answer this day. Tell me this: What would ye do unto one who wittingly, and not in battle but shamefully, slew your father, and he innocent, even such a man, say, as Kian the Noble?"

There was no whisper of answer. All sat there amazed, marvelling at the strange question. But at last Nuadh the King spoke.

"What meaning lives in thy words, Ildanna? For we know that thy father Kian is not slain, for he was not in the Great Battle."

"Nevertheless he is slain, and here in this

royal place my eyes behold them who slew him."

When Lu of the Long Hand had spoken these words, every man looked from neighbour to neighbour in amaze. But all waited for the king to speak.

"What sayest thou, Nuadh of the Silver Hand, Ardree of Erin?"

"I have this to say, that if a man wittingly, and without the just cause of war, slew my father, and he innocent, I would not be content with exacting death, but would rather lop him limb from limb daily till he died."

"And what say ye, chiefs and nobles of the Dedannan race?"

"We say as the Ardree says," cried one and all, save the three who sat on golden-knobbed seats near the high king, though these too bowed their heads in acquiescence.

"And what say ye, ye sons of Turenn?"

At this all turned and looked upon Brian and Ur and Urba, who sat pale and stern. Brian answered for himself and his brothers.

"We say as the high king says."

"Nuadh of the Silver Hand, Ardree of Erin, and all ye chieftains and chiefs and nobles of the Dedannan race, I call ye to witness that this man who has spoken slew my father, and that he and his brothers are jointly guilty of that foul deed."

For more than the furthest singing of an arrow, there was silence. Neither the king nor any man spoke, but all looked to the sons of Turenn to say Yea or Nay. But Brian and Ur and Urba sat in a frozen stillness, and moved neither their hands nor their lips, and stared only with unwavering eyes upon the white accusing face of the son of the murdered Kian.

Then Lu spoke again.

"Behold the men who slew my father. And now, O king, I say not whether there were good cause for this slaying : all men know that there was a feud between the clans of Kian and Turenn. Nor do I wish to bring evil into this house and town of thine. Because one man is dead, there is no need that others must die who have nought to do with his death. I have come in peace : I would go in peace. But this only I say : I go not hence till I have won from the sons of Turenn the vow of my eric."

"That is right and wise," answered the

king, "and for myself I would be well content if, being guilty, I could evade death by paying any eric whatsoever."

At this Brian rose.

"Lu, son of Kian, has spoken inadvisedly, O king. He has accused us of a crime, he knowing nothing of when or how that deed was done, and in what circumstances, and how made inevitable. Nor, again, have we ever admitted that we are guilty of this deed of murder."

"It is enough. Kian, father of Lu Ildanna, came to his death through ye three sons of Turenn. Whatsoever eric Lu may exact, that eric ye shall have to pay. Otherwise the lives that ye hold so dear, being your own, will no longer have the shelter of this royal place ; and as no man's hand can be raised to aid thee, ye shall be at the mercy of Lu of the Long Hand, and of whomsoever he may bring against thee."

For a brief while Brian talked low with his brothers ; then he turned and addressed Nuadh the king and Lu Lamfada.

"We are for peace, not strife. We say not we are guilty, but we will pay the eric that Lu, son of Kian, may demand, save only that it be not against the life of Turenn our father."

"That is well said," exclaimed Nuadh of the Silver Hand.

"I accept the troth," said Lu, "and now call upon all here to witness that the sons of Turenn have made a solemn pledge."

There were few there who did not wonder what the eric would be, for all knew that Lu was a stern man, and would not rest till he had done his utmost to make the sons of Turenn expiate their deed.

Great was their amazement, therefore, when Lu gave forth the eric that he demanded.

"The eric I demand is this," he said : "that ye bring me three apples, a certain skin, a spear, two horses and a chariot, seven swine, a hound, and a roasting spit. And further, that ye shout three shouts upon a hill. Yet, if ye will," Lu added scornfully, "I shall remit a portion of this eric if ye find it too heavy for ye."

"It is neither heavy nor great," answered Brian, "if there be no hidden evil behind. For by the Sun and Wind I swear that I would not count too heavy an eric, three hundreds of thousands of apples, or thrice a hundred skins, or many score horses and chariots, spears and hounds, or a shouting a hundred times upon a hundred hills."

" Nevertheless, I do not account it small," answered Lu gravely. " But give me now security that ye shall fulfil this eric to the uttermost."

" We give ourselves as security."

" Not so," exclaimed Lu scornfully. " I will not have the security of thyselves."

" Then I call upon Bove Derg, son of the Dagda, and upon Nuadh of the Silver Hand, Ardree of Erin, and upon the score I shall name of the foremost chiefs of the Dedannan race, to be our pledge and warranty."

And after Brian had named the score, all they, and Nuadh the king, and Bove Derg, the son of the Dagda, gave the pledge, so that thenceforth the sons of Turenn were under solemn *geas* to fulfil the eric, or die in the effort to fulfil that eric, or otherwise bring dishonour upon all these noble and great lords, each of whom moreover would be bound to seek the lives of Brian and Ur and Urba.

" And now tell us if that is all, O Lu Ildanna, for much I misdoubt me if thou hast no evil thought for us behind thy fair-seeming words."

Thereat all leaned forward and listened eagerly, for each man knew that Lu was not vainly called the Ildanna, for there was no one in all Erin who had so much knowledge, or whose craft was so greatly to be feared. When he had uttered the eric that he demanded, all were at first amazed. Then some had thought that he was under *geas* never to exact a great eric, but always the smallest that he might make ; but most were troubled, for behind these slight exactions they knew that he had arrowy intentions.

"Yes, ye sons of Turenn," Lu Lamfada began slowly, "I shall tell ye now what my eric is. I do not think ye shall find it over easy."

Brian and Ur and Urba rose, but all the host otherwise remained seated. The three sons of Turenn leaned upon their spears, and tall and goodly warriors they seemed, and worthy of their great fame as three of the seven chief champions of Erin.

"First, then, there is this. The skin I demand of ye is one that belongs to the king of Greece in the far eastern lands. It is the skin of healing. No man need die of wounds who has that skin ; and cold water, too, it will make into wine. I do not think ye will come easily by that skin.

" Second, there is this. The spear I demand of ye is the spear called Aradvar, the dreadful spear of Pisarr, Prince of Persia, whose point is for ever kept cooling in a cauldron of water, so terrible is its fiery thirst, and that thirst for blood. I do not think ye will find the spear of Pisarr easy to obtain.

" Third, there is this. The chariot and two horses that I demand of ye belong to Dobar, the king of Sicily. They heed neither the rough ways of the land nor the rough ways of the sea, but travel equally and at the will of him who drives. I do not think ye will find it easy to obtain that chariot and its two horses.

" Further, there is this. Far to the south there is a great lord, Asol of the Golden Pillars. It is he who owns the seven swine I ask of ye. Ye may slay the seven and yet all will remain. They know not death, though ye may slao them and feed upon them. There is no death upon them. I do not think ye will find it easy to obtain these swine.

" Fifth, there is this.  In a further land still, that is called Irrua, there is a great and terrible hound named Falinnish.  So fierce is he that whatever beast comes within sight of him falls in helpless fear.  I do not think ye will find that hound very easy to obtain, or bring with ye from far-off Irrua.

" Sixth, there is this.  In the remote seas is an isle called Fiancarya.  It is there that the sea-women dwell.  In caverns beneath the waves they roast their food.  It is their roasting spit I ask of ye.  I do not think ye will find it easy to obtain that thing.

" Seventh, there is this.  The three apples I ask of ye are of gold, and are in an ancient garden in Isberna.  That ancient close is well guarded, O Sons of Turenn, so that ye may not find it easy even to see the wind-waved summits of the trees.  I do not think ye will bring back these apples.[1]

" And lastly, there is this.  In the remotest north of remote Lochlin there is a hill called Mekween.  It is so called from a man of that name who lives there.  He is a great and

---

[1] Probably Isberna is Hispania (Spain), and the apples the golden apples of the Hesperides.

powerful man, and none others equal him save only his two sons. So terrible are they that no man dare venture into that wild place where they live, save in amity. It was with them that my father learned his great craft with the sword; and so great will their wrath be that ye have slain him, that even were I to forgive ye, they would not. Moreover, Mekween and his sons are under *geas* not to allow a shout to be shouted upon that hill. I do not think ye will find it easy to pass the sons of Mekween, nor to shout three shouts upon that hill."

With that, Lu the Ildanna bowed before the king, and sat upon his golden chair again.

All men looked with sorrow upon the sons of Turenn. Any of the seven *geasan* of this eric that Lu put upon them was more than enough for any hero: how then would they survive till the last, or, having survived, how would they bring back with them these things, and how escape the wrath of Mekween and his sons?

Nevertheless, the sons of Turenn were now under bond, and they had no choice but to do what they could to fulfil their eric.

With sad hearts they left the great beauty and wonder of Tara, and with sadder hearts still reached their own land. Here with sorrow they bade farewell to Turenn their father and to dark-eyed Enya their sister, whom they loved so passing well, and to all their kindred and folk. Thereafter they set forth on their long and ever more and more perilous quest.

It would have been easy for the sons of Turenn to have passed over into Alba, and sought service with the king of that country; or to have gone among the Kymri in the in-land highlands beyond the isle where Manan-nan had his home : or southward to Lyonesse or into Armorica. But honour is a better thing than ease, and it would ill have befit heroes such as Brian and Ur and Urba to have evaded their solemn troth. A bitter wrong they had done, because of the heredi-tary feud betwixt the clans of Turenn and Kian : but now there was one thing only to do, and that to fulfil the eric put upon them by Lu, son of Kian. Moreover, Nuadh the Ardree and Bove Derg, son of the Dagda, and a score of the noblest lords in Erin were their warranty that they would do this thing.

So, one day of the days, they set forth from Erin : and sad indeed were they when across the foam they took their last look at Dun Turenn and at the dear familiar hill of Ben Edar.

For that night Peterkin heard no more of the story of the Fate of the Sons of Turenn; but all the next evening, and the next again, he sat entranced by the strange moving tale of how Brian and Ur and Urba one by one fulfilled the hard and perilous conditions of their eric, and this until the sixth was done.

But here, now, this tale cannot be told in full. To tell it aright would need a volume not less than this is.

It must suffice that after innumerable hardships, after fierce cold and fiercer heat, after hunger and thirst and daily perils by land or sea, and strange and frightful encounters, and hazardous fights with monsters and wild men and kings and princes, the sons of Turenn found themselves sailing towards the remote north of Lochlin, having accomplished the six seeming impossible conditions.

That nigh-impossible task, indeed, had been made possible by the magic boat of Manannan, called the Sweeper of the Waves, which they had won from Lu by unlooked-for wile. For before they had left Tara they had played a game of chess with Lu Ildanna, well knowing that Lu was under *geas* never to refuse to play at chess when asked by any Dedannan, or to pay the hazard that was decided upon, whatsoever it might be. There was no player in all Erin to surpass Ur, though few knew this, for he was little given to talk, and still less of his own doings.

First Urba had offered to play with Lu, and the hazard of that play was to be the life of Lu Ildanna. "I will play that hazard," he said, "if thou wilt pay the like penalty if thou dost lose." But when Urba refused, he could play no more, because he had declined the counter-hazard.

Then Brian had offered to play, and the hazard of that play was to be Daurya, the beautiful daughter of a great lord, whom Lu loved. "I will play that hazard," he said, "if, in return, thou wilt pledge me Enya of the Dark Eyes, thy sister." But when Brian refused this hazard, he too could play no more with Lu until Lu asked him.

Then Ur played, and the hazard of that

play was the "Sweeper of the Waves," Manannan's magic boat. "I will play that hazard," Lu said, "if in return thou wilt sail in it, and affront Manannan to his face." To that Ur agreed, and they played, and Ur won.

This magic boat would sail swiftly and safely in any sea whether calm or tempest-wrought, and at a word would make for any coast or haven; more like a great bird it was, or some creature of the air and sea.

"White shall be thy foamy track," cried Lu as they sailed away; "but red everywhere shall be the wake behind ye."

And so it was. For death and the bitterness of the sword were ever in their way and in their wake. Nevertheless, they unceasingly rejoiced in their possession of the Sweeper of the Waves, and when their ericquest took them into far eastern lands beyond the reach of great rivers, they hid their precious vessel, or bade it lie till it heard their summoning voice.

And so at the last it happened that the sons of Turenn won the three golden apples out of the guarded close in Isberna; and by craft and daring carried away from Sicily the famous chariot and two steeds which had no peer in all the world; and from Asol of the Golden Pillars, who gave them in ransom for his life, they took the seven deathless swine; and from its cauldron in the heart of a hostile city they snatched the terrible spear of Pisarr; and the far-famed skin of healing they brought away from the palace of Toosh, king of Greece, whose head they left idly rolling upon his marble floor; and in far Irrua they put captivity upon the terrible hound Falinnish; and in the wild seas of Fiancarya they dared the sea-women in their caverns under the waves, and took from them the roasting spit that Lu had demanded.

All this they did, and much else in the doing of these wonders. And now nothing remained but to shout three shouts upon the hill of Mekween; and to this end they sailed blithely and swiftly towards the far north of Lochlin.

But meanwhile, in far-away Erin, Lu Ildanna became aware, by his subtle magic and knowledge, that the sons of Turenn had one by one accomplished all but the last of the bitter tasks of the eric he had set upon them. He had not deemed this fulfilment possible, but while greatly he marvelled that courage and endurance could so bring impossible things to pass, he dreaded lest the sons of Turenn should prevail in the last task also. For if they came back to Erin with all that great eric fulfilled, then would there be a blood-shedding terrible indeed.

Moreover, Lu Ildanna, who saw far ahead of the things of the moment, was even now preparing for that second great battle upon the Plain of Moytura which he knew would come again ; and a battle mightier and more desperate than the last, or than ever was seen in Erin before. Great warrior as he was, and lordly as was the war-host of the Dedannans, he feared this final battle unless he had at least half of the eric he had set upon the sons of Turenn—and, above all, the Spear of Pisarr, the Skin of Healing, and the War-chariot of the Sicilian king. Therefore he longed for the return of his foes, the sons of Turenn ; yet feared that they should come back having accomplished all.

So on a day of the days he made a deep and potent spell, and sent this spell forth to work its noiseless and invisible way across land and sea and under the flaming sun and the white glister of the stars, till it should find the Sweeper of the Waves.

So forth that subtle spell went, and when it reached at last the Sweeper of the Waves it crawled stealthily into the great boat, and wound itself about the weary bodies of Brian and Ur and Urba, and moved into their brains, filled as they were with dreams of Erin and of home.

The spell was the spell of oblivion, but they knew it not.

And so it chanced that they could no longer understand why it was they sailed northward, nor had they any memory of the last obligation of the eric, and thought neither of Mekween and his sons, nor of the doom put upon them by Lu, nor of the vanity of all their long quest and brave endurance if they returned with the eric unfulfilled in the least part.

It was with joy that they set their prow for green Erin; and with joy that they saw again its green grassy hills above its white shores; and with joy that they recognised Ben Edar and Dun Turenn; and with joy that they kissed once more Turenn their father and Enya of the Dark Eyes, their sister, and knew themselves back at last from all their weary wandering and endless peril and strife.

Great was the marvelling at what they brought back, and the oldest druids admitted that never in the history of Erin had so great a wonder been done.

Alas! theirs was but a brief joy.

Lu Ildanna said nothing till he had put away all the treasures of that eric. Then he said gravely :

" All is accomplished save one thing. Have ye shouted three shouts upon the hill of Mekween ?"

And as he spoke he broke the spell, so that suddenly Brian and Ur and Urba remembered, and with shame and grief had to say that this last thing they had not done.

In vain did Turenn supplicate for his sons, in vain even was the pleading of the king. Lu had but one answer. " All else is as nought if they have not done this thing—to shout three shouts upon the hill of Mekween."

So once more the sore-tried heroes set forth, but with dim presentiments of woe ; for now they had neither the Skin of Healing nor the Sweeper of the Waves, for these had been taken away by Lu, and he would not give them again.

Nevertheless, they reached their goal. A great and terrible fight was theirs with Mekween and his sons Conn and Corc and Ae— the most terrible fight, the old bards say, which was ever fought between six men—for at the beginning the sons of Turenn slew Mekween.

At dusk on that disastrous day six gashed and mutilated men lay in the swoon of death. Out of that swoon, three men never waked, and these were Conn and Corc and Ae: and two had not strength to move even when they waked, and these were Ur and Urba; and Brian alone staggered to his feet, and stared through a mist of blood.

When at last the eldest of the sons of Turenn looked upon his brothers, and saw their glassy eyes staring idly at the sunrise, he feared that they too were dead. Then he saw that the pulse of life still flickered. Weak as he was, he took first Ur upon his shoulders, and bore him up the rocky slope to the ridge of the hill of Mekween; and then returned and bore Urba thither also.

Then it was that three thin, faint shouts

went forth upon the hill, so thin and faint that the browsing stags on the uplands did not lift their heads.

Thus was it that the Great Eric was fulfilled.

But, alas! the piteous tale of their return. None could tell aright that woe-stricken, death-weary voyage of three dying men, upborne by one hope only—that they might free their name and clan from the eric put upon them, and lay their accusing deaths at the feet of Lu Ildanna.

Yet hardly might they do even this. For as they drew nigh the coasts of Erin once more, Ur and Urba spoke to Brian and supplicated him to raise their heads, so that, before they died, they might see again the green hills of their beloved Banba, and high Ben Edar, and their home Dun Turenn.

But to this Brian made answer :

" Dear brothers, too great is my weakness, for I am now even as ye are. Lo! through my gaping wounds one of these birds that skim above us might fly, and be not snared within me."

After that, they spake no word till the galley grided against the sands of Erin.

Soon all in Dun Turenn and in all the lands

of Edar knew that Brian, Ur, and Urba were come again ; but sorrowful were they indeed to see, instead of the three proud heroes, only three wasted men like unto shadows. Neither Ur nor Urba could speak, but Brian's voice could rise to a thin whisper.

With halting breath he bade his father hasten to Tara, and tell Lu Lamfada that now all the eric was paid at last ; and then beseech him, by his honour and fair name, and for the glory of the old Dedannan faith, and by the invocation of the Sun and Moon and Wind, to lend to the three perishing sons of Turenn, the Skin of Healing, so that their lives might not flicker out as the flame of spent torches.

But, alas ! Lu would not yield to that prayer, not even when the grey hairs of Turenn were at his feet. Then once more Brian besought his father ; and now it was that he bade his father put him upon a litter, and bear him gently, because of his open wounds, and lay him at the feet of Lu.

And when he was there, Brian said this thing :

"Behold, O Lu Ildanna, son of Kian, we have fulfilled the heaviest eric ever exacted of any man since the world was made. And now we ask this one thing alone : one hour only of the Healing Skin that we ourselves brought unto thee. Yet not for myself I ask this, if thou desirest my life, since it was I who slew thy father, but for my brothers Ur and Urba. And if not for them—though they are guiltless of this ill, and are with me in this dire plight because they would not forsake me, but made my fortune their fortune—then for the sake of the old hero Turenn, who was comrade in arms with thy father Kian when both were youths. And by the Sun, and by the Moon, and by the Wind, and by thine honour, I cry to thee to be merciful, and to do this thing."

But Lu smiled a bitter, evil smile. Half that smile was from the cruel revengefulness in his breast, and half because he feared that if Brian and Ur and Urba lived, there would be an end of the Dedannan race, for the fierce internecine wars which would be in Erin.

" I would not give thee the Skin, Brian, though all thy race, nay, not though every man and woman in the eastlands were to perish with thee. Go hence, and in the shadow of death remember the eric unto death of Lu the Long-Handed."

So Brian went forth upon his litter, with the death-sweat already upon him.

That night a long and bitter lamentation went up from Dun Turenn, and the Beacons of Death flared upon Ben Edar. For, at the setting of the sun, Brian and Ur and Urba breathed out their souls into the light, and these moved swift to Flathinnis, the holy island where are gathered all the souls of heroes.

Yet on their way to join the innumerous deathless dead, they halted once, for they heard a thin voice crying upon the wind. It was the voice of Turenn their father.

In one great grave before the mighty dun, the four were buried, erect, and sword in hand. And on a slab midway in the vast cairn of stones that was erected thereon, was writ in branching Ogam the names and glory of Turenn and his three sons. For three days the people wept. Then, as the wont was, Enya of the Dark Eyes decreed the funeral games.

And so these heroes died, and with them went the third part of the perishing glory of the Tuatha-De-Danann.

For in the end, that which is to be, is.   There is no gainsaying the slow, sure word of Fate. And, too, there is this thing to be said. The wind in the grass outlasts the branching Ogam graven in granite, and the granite ceno-taph itself, and the powdered dust of that granite.

# Darthool and the
# Sons of Usna

"the story this
Of her, the morning star of loveliness,
Unhappy Helen of a western land."

"*Deirdrê.*"   *Trs. by Dr. Douglas Hyde.*

A great raven, glossy black, and burnished in the
sun rays.

To face p. 177.]

# Darthool and the
# Sons of Usna

THE story I will tell you now, Peterkin, is more beautiful, though not so old.

In all the regions of the Gael throughout Scotland, and in every isle, from Arran and Islay in the south, to Iona in the west, and Tiree in mid-sea, and the Outer Hebrides, there is no story of the old far-off days so well known as that of Darthool.

She it is who in Ireland is called Deirthrê or Deirdrê; and in Ireland to this day there is not a cowherd who has not heard of Deirdrê.

Her beauty filled the old world of the Gael with a sweet, wonderful, and abiding rumour. The name of Deirdrê has been as a lamp to a thousand poets. In a land of heroes and brave and beautiful women, how shall one name survive? Yet to this day and for ever, men will remember Deirdrê, the torch of men's thoughts, and Grainne whom Diarmid loved and died for, and Maev who ruled mightily, and Fand whose white feet trod faery dew, and many another. For beauty is the most excellent sweet thing in all the world, and though of it a few perish, and a myriad die from knowing nothing of it, beneath it the nations of men move forward as their one imperishable star. Therefore he who adds to the beauty of the world is of the sons of God. He who destroys or debases beauty is of the darkness, and shall have darkness for his reward.

The day will come, Peterkin, when you will find a rare and haunting music in these names. They will bring you a lost music, a lost world, and imperishable beauty. You will dwell with them, till you love Deirdrê as did the sons of Usna, and would die for her, or live to see her starry eyes; till you look longingly upon the Grainne of your dreams, and cry as Diarmid did, when he asked her, as death menaced them, if even yet she would go back, and she answered that she would not: "Then go forward, O Grainne!"

Many poets and shennachies have related

this tale. I have heard it given now this way, and now that ; sometimes with new names and scenes, sometimes with other beginnings and endings ; but at heart it is ever the same. Nor does it matter whether the father of Deirdrê be Felim, the warrior bard of the Ultonians, or Malcolm the Harper, or any other, or whether the fair and sweet beauty of the world be called Deirdrê or Darthool. But as here in our own land she is called Darthool, that I will call her.

I will tell the story as it is told in the old chronicles, and to this day, and if I add aught to it, that shall only be what I myself heard when I was young, and had from the lips of an old woman, Barabal Mac-Aodh, who was my nurse. She came out of Tiree or Coll, I forget which.

Well, in the ancient dim days when Emania was the capital of the Ultonians, the fair and wonderful capital of the kingdom of Ulster, and before Maev, the queen of the south, had buried the chivalry of the north in dust and blood, there came into the realm of Concobar the Ultonian king, whom some call Conor and some Connachar, three of the noblest and fairest of the youths of the world. These are they who then bore, and in all the years since have borne, the name of the Sons of Usna, who was himself, some say, a feudal king, in Alba.[1]

It is because of these three heroes that this story I am relating is often called the story of the Sons of Usna. But first, I have that to tell you which precedes the time when Nathos,[2] and Ailne, and Ardan, stood in the house of Concobar the high king.

This Concobar was a great prince. He was known as Concobar MacNessa, for though he was the son of Fatna the Wise, son of Ross the Red, son of Rory, Nessa his mother was a famous queen, and had indeed by her beauty and her wiles brought Concobar to the over-lordship of Uladh[3] when he was yet a youth.

In many of the tales of the old far-off days, you will hear the rumour of the splendour and wonder of the city of Emania. In Concobar's time it was called Emain Macha, for it had been built by a great and beautiful queen—Macha Mongruay, Macha of the Ruddy Hair. A thousand times have poets chanted of Emain Macha, and in the ancient days the bards

---

[1] *Alba.* That is, Gaelic Scotland, and in particular Argyll.

[2] *Naois* in the old Irish Gaelic.          [3] Ulster.

loved to sing also of Macha herself.   Here is
an old far-off lay :

"O 'tis a good house, and a palace fair, the dun of Macha,
And happy with a great household is Macha there ;
Druids she had, and bards, minstrels, harpers, knights,
Hosts of servants she had, and wonders beautiful and rare,
But nought so wonderful and sweet as her face, queenly
      fair,
          O Macha of the Ruddy Hair !

The colour of her great dun is the shining whiteness of
      lime,
And within it are floors strewn with green rushes and
      couches white,
Soft wondrous silks and blue gold-claspt mantles and furs
Are there, and jewelled golden cups for revelry by night :
Thy grianan of gold and glass is filled with sunshine-light,
          O Macha, queen by day, queen by night !

Beyond the green portals, and the brown and red thatch of
      wings
Striped orderly, the wings of innumerous stricken birds,
A wide shining floor reaches from wall to wall, wondrously
      carven
Out of a sheet of silver, whereon are graven swords
Intricately ablaze ; mistress of many hoards
          Art thou, Macha of few words !

Fair indeed is thy couch, but fairer still is thy throne,
A chair it is, all of a blaze of wonderful yellow gold :
There thou sittest, and watchest the women going to and
      fro,
Each in garments fair and with long locks twisted fold in
      fold :

With the joy that is in thy house men would not grow old,
    O Macha, proud, austere, cold.

Of a surety there is much joy to be had of thee and thine,
There in the song-sweet sunlit bowers in that place :
Wounded men might sink in sleep and be well content
So to sleep, and to dream perchance, and know no other
    grace
Than to wake and look betimes on thy proud queenly face,
    O Macha of the Proud Face !

And if there be any here who wish to know more of this
    wonder,
Go, you will find all as I have shown, as I have said :
From beneath its portico thatched with wings of birds blue
    and yellow
Reaches a green lawn, where a fount is fed
From crystal and gems : of crystal and gold each bed
        In the house of Macha of the Ruddy Head.

In that great house where Macha the queen has her pleas-
    aunce
There is everything in the whole world that a man might
    desire.
God is my witness that if I say little it is for this,
That I am grown faint with wonder, and can no more
    admire,
But say this only, that I live and die in the fire
        Of thine eyes, O Macha, my desire,
        With thine eyes of fire ! " [1]

---

[1] This song, adapted to Macha, is founded upon a portion
of the poem by Coel O'Neamhain, in honour of a beautiful
queen named Crede, as translated by Professor Sullivan
and others.

It was in this wonderful forefront of Ulster that Concobar reigned. The fame of Emain Macha was throughout Gaeldom ; and there was no man or woman who, as the days went by, did not hear of the greatness of Concobar.

On a day of the days, the king went with his chief lords on a visit to the dun of Felim, a warrior and harper whom he loved. There was to be great feasting, and all men were glad. Felim himself rejoiced, though he would fain have had the king come to him a few days later, for his wife was heavy with child, and looked for her hour that very day or the next.

In the midmost of the feast, Concobar saw that Cathba, an aged Druid who had accompanied him, was staring into the other world that is about us.

"Speak, Cathba," he said. "There is no man in all Erin who has wisdom like unto thine. What is it that thou seest, with the inner sight that I perceive well is now upon thee?"

"Old as I am with the heavy burden of years and sorrow, O Concobar, did I not beg that I might come with thee to this festival at the dun of Felim? And that was not because I wearied to hear strange harping and singing;

good and fine and better than our own as this harping is here, in the house of Felim ; for I am old and weary, and care more to listen to the wind in the grass, or to the sighing upon the hill, than to any music of war or love."

"Then what was it that was in thy mind, Cathba ?"

"This, O king. I saw a shadow arise whenever I thought of our Ultonian realm, and I felt within me the burden of a new prophecy. Nevertheless, I was moved by naught till I entered the dun of Felim, and now I know."

"Speak," said the king; while all there listened with awe as well as eagerness, for Cathba was the wisest of the Druids, and knew many mysteries, and what he had foretold had ever come to pass. Slowly, the white-haired Druid looked around the faces of all seated there. Then he looked at the king. Then he looked at Felim.

"To thee, O Felim, shall be born this night a sting, a sword, a battering-ram, and a flame."

Felim the Harper stared with intent gaze, but said nothing. Of what avail to say aught against the decrees of the gods ?

"This night shall that which I have said be born unto thee, O Felim. The sting will sting

to madness him who is king of the Ultonians ;
the sword will sever from Uladh the chief of
her glories, the proud Red Branch for which
Concobar and all his chivalry shall perish ; the
ram shall batter down the proud splendour of
Emain Macha ; the flame shall pass from dun
to dun, from forest to forest, from hill to hill,
from the isles of Ara on the west to the shores
of the sea-stream of the Moyle on the north,
and to those of the sea of Manannan in the east."

Still Felim answered nothing.   Then the
king spoke :

"Thy words come in dust, like wind-whirled
autumn leaves.   We have not thy further sight,
Cathba, and understand thee not."

Then once more Cathba spake out of the
dream that was upon him :

"Two stars I see shining in a web of dusk ;
and, in the shadow of that dusk, a low tower of
ivory and white pearls I see, and a strange crimson fruit ; and through all and over all I hear the
low, sweet vibration of the strings of a harp, a
harp such as the Dedannan folk play upon in
the moonshine in lonely places, but sweeter
still, sweeter and more wonderful."

"Is this thy second vision one and the same
with thy first, O Cathba ?" asked the king.

"Even so. For the shining stars are her eyes, and the web of dusk is the flower-fragrant maze of her hair, that low tower of ivory is her fair, white, wonderful neck, and her white teeth are these pearls, and that strange crimson fruit is no other than her smiling mouth—a little smiling mouth with life and death upon it because of its laughter and grave stillness. As for that harp-playing, it is her voice I hear—a voice more soft and sweet and tender than the love-music of Angus Ogue himself. O shining eyes, O strange crimson fruit that is a little smiling mouth, O sweet voice that is more excellent to hear than the wild music of the Hidden People of the hills—it is of ye, of ye that I speak, and of thee, O tender, delicate fawn, in all thy loveliness."

None spake, but all stared at the Druid. For dream was upon them at these words, and each man imagined his desire, and was wrought by it, and was rapt in strange longing.

It was Concobar who broke the silence.

"Of whomsoever thou speakest, Cathba, she is surely of the divine folk. That exceeding loveliness is for the joy or the sorrow of the world."

Only Felim the Harper was troubled, for now he knew well that the ancient Druid spoke of the unborn child with whom even then his wife was in travail. But no sooner had Concobar ceased than Cathba rose, with his great dark eyes aflame beneath his white eye-brows. His voice was loud and terrible.

" Behold, I see this thing ; behold the vision of Cathba the Druid, who is old and nigh unto death. And what is before mine eyes is a sea, a sea of flowing crimson, a sea of blood. Foaming it rises, and wells forth, and overflows, and drowns great straths and valleys, and laves the flanks of high hills, and from the summits of mountains pours down upon the lands of the Gael in a thundering flood, blood-red to the blood-red sea."

But now the spell of silence was broken. All leaped to their feet, and many put their hands upon their swords. There was not one who did not fear the prophesying of Cathba the wise Druid. That deluge of blood, was it not a terror, a great ruin to avert ?

"If this child that the wife of Felim the Harper is to bear this night be a blood-bringer so terrible," they cried, "let us slay her at birth. For surely it is better to kill a child than to destroy a nation."

So spake they out of their ignorance that they thought wisdom. For they did not know that there is no thought, no power, no spell, no craft, wherewith to turn aside the feet of Destiny. What has to be, will be, and no man living can say or do aught that is of avail against the inevitable tides of Fate.

For the first time since Cathba had prophesied, Felim uttered word.

" Listen, my kinsmen and fellow-knights of the Red Branch. A sore pity is it for my wife Elva to bear a daughter that shall be a sting to sting the king to madness, and a sword to sever the Red Branch from Uladh, our fair heritage, and a ram to break down the walls of Emania, and a flame to consume the land from shore to shore. And as for that sea of blood, let it not be upon my head. For I, the father of the child of Elva, that Cathba says is to be a woman-child and of a beauty wonderful to see, say unto ye : That which ye would fain do, do. If it seems good unto ye, O Concobar, and ye of the Red Branch, let this child perish, so that the doom foretold by Cathba may be averted."

At that all were glad save Concobar. Two men was he, this king: a man who recked little of aught save his desire, and a man who had wisdom. Out of his wisdom he knew that Felim and the Red Branch lords spoke madness, for if it was ordained that the child of Elva should bring doom, that doom would surely come. Out of his longing he loved the beauty of which Cathba had spoken, and desired it against the years to come, and for the solace of his years when he had loved much and at the last was fain only of that which was the crown of life. So he spoke to those before him, and prevailed with them. Not vainly was he called Concobar of the Honeymouth.

"I will speak first to thee, Felim, son of Dall, my bard. It is not good to put death upon the fruit of one's loins. Thine own child should not see death through thee. But even were it so, it is not meet for me or for any one to bring the shame and pain of death to the house of a friend. Therefore, do not speak of putting silence and darkness upon the child of Elva."

Having spoken thus, the king turned to the lords of the Red Branch. As the wont was, at the royal festivals there were five and three score over three hundred of the Red Branch there and then.[1]

"And to ye, Ultonians, I say this thing also. Do not bring blood into the hospitable home of Felim; that would be a stain upon him, upon ye yourselves, and upon me the king. But this is my counsel. Let the child live. There is no good in idle blood, and if ye stain yourselves with it, there shall be greater loss and sorrow to follow. Ye are all grown men, and not boys who do not know our laws. Ye know the Law of the Eric. Well, I will free ye of all doom, for upon my head be it. To myself I will take this fair child, and upon me, and not upon the Ultonians, nor upon the Red Branch, nor upon any other whomsoever save Concobar MacNessa, the high king, be the penalty, if penalty there be."

At that a son of a king arose.

"That is well, O Concobar. But what of Cathba's prophecy? We do not wish to see

---

[1] Given as in the Gaelic: *ciugear agus tri fichead agus tri chead.* Large numbers are in Gaelic invariably built up thus (instead of, for example, as here, four hundred and sixty). In an old Irish-Gaelic version the particular number here is given as "five and three score above six hundred and one thousand" (*i.e.,* 1,760).

the sting that shall sting thee to madness, and if the child live shall we not see that sting?"

"Of that I have thought, that I have foreseen, Congal, son of Rossa of the Lakes. For I shall send the child into a lonely place, and there in a solitary rath shall she dwell and grow in years, and no man shall look upon her save I myself, and that only in the fulness of time. She shall be solitary and apart as the Crane of Innisbea, that has dwelt upon its isle since the world was made, and is seen of none."

"Tell us once more, Concobar MacNessa; dost thou take this child, and the doom of this child unto thee, and to thee alone?"

"I have sworn. She shall grow in years, and be wife to me when the time is come. And if sorrow come with her, that sorrow shall be my sorrow. Not upon Uladh be it, but upon me. I have spoken."

"And as for thee, Felim?"

"It would be better to slay the child than to drown the land in blood."

"And as for thee, Cathba?"

"There is but one law: that which has to come, cometh." But while they were thus debating, the loud chanting voices of women were heard, and soon a messenger came, crying loudly that a child had been born to Elva, wife of Felim, and that it was a woman-child, and exceeding comely, and strong, and white as milk.

Once more Cathba the Druid spoke.

" She shall be called Darthool,[1] this woman whose beauty shall be a flame, and whose eyes shall be as stars."

And so it was. The child was spared, and that night Elva slept in peace, and for many nights.

When the days of the feasting were over, Concobar left the dun of Felim, and returned with all his company to Emania. With him he took the little child Darthool, and Elva came with him for a month and a day.

The month and the day soon passed, and then Elva went back to her own place. It was the will of the high king and of Felim, her husband ; nevertheless, she sorrowed to part with her little child, who, even as a breast-babe, had eyes of so great a beauty that it was a joy to look into them.

[1] In old Irish Gaelic, *Derdriu*, then *Deirdrê*, sometimes *Darethra*. In Scotland, *Dearduil* (pronounced Dart'-weel, Darth-uil, or " Darthool," whence Macpherson's " Darthula," who rather loosely says the name is *Dart'huile*, a woman of beautiful eyes). The oldest name is said to signify alarm.

Before the year was over—for, according to what Cathba the wise Druid said, the child must either be slain or hidden away before the first year of her life were past—Concobar sent Darthool with the nursing woman to whom he entrusted her, to a small *lios*, or fort, deep in the heart of the royal forest. A ban was upon that forest that none might hunt or even stray there without the king's will ; and now that ban was made absolute, and it was known that death would be the portion of any man who went under these branches. None was to enter that woodland save Concobar, or whosoever might be of his chosen company, or whom the king might thither lead.

Concobar himself saw that food and milk was sent in plenty to the lios, and once in every seven days he went thither himself. As year after year passed the secret of the hiding-place of Darthool went out of men's minds, and none knew of the lios save the king, and the sister of the nursing woman, who was his own foster-child and under *geas* or bond to him. This woman was named Lavarcam (*Leabharcham*), and was fair to see, and whom Concobar held to be discreet and trustworthy beyond any other of his own people. She was of the royal

household, and of the women trained as chroni-
clers and relaters.[1]

The little starry-eyed babe grew to a child,
and from a child to a fawn of a girl, fair to see,
and from a young girl to a maid, of a beauty so
great that Concobar knew when she came to
full womanhood she would be indeed as Cathba
the Druid had prophesied.

Darthool saw no one but her nurse, and
the tutor whom the king had sent to teach
her all that could be taught, and not only in
learning, but in courtesy and nobility; and
Lavarcam, who alone went to and fro.  From
the time that Darthool passed out of her first
girlhood the king saw little of her, but twice
in each year—at the Festival of the Sun in
the time of the greening, and at the Festival
of end Summer at the fall of the leaf; and this
because of a warning that had been given
him by Cathba the ancient Druid.

How can the beauty of so fair and sweet a
woman be revealed?   Her loveliness was even
as Cathba had foretold.   It was a surpassing

---

[1] The Gaelic original is *Beanchaointeach* (*Banchainte*)
*Conchubhar fein*, etc., and means literally Concobar's Con-
versation-woman, which perhaps might be rendered as
" gossip."

loveliness, and the three women who saw her often marvelled at it, and wondered no more that Darthool should be kept apart, for of a surety she would be a torch to put flame into the hearts of men, and to set great duns and raths and towered capitals and warring nations ablaze. The poets have sung of her, and no man has sung but out of his deep desire. Her great sad eyes, so full of dream, were blue as are the hill-tarns at noon, and often dusky as they when passing clouds put purple into their depths; and like a golden web her hair was, sprayed out with shining light, wonderful, glorious; and her rowan-red lips were indeed that strange crimson fruit which Cathba had foreseen—rowan-red against the cream-white softness of her skin. Cream-white her body was, and her neck like a tower of ivory; slim and graceful was she as a fawn, and fleet of foot as the wild roes on the hills, and when she moved in the sunlight or the shadow she was so beautiful that tears came at times to the eyes of the women in that lonely place. Yet even more wonderful was her voice—low and sweet and with music in it, like the whisper of the wind among the reeds, or the ripple of green leaves, or the murmuring of a brook.

But now and from this time forth Concobar did not see her. For a year and a day after she attained womanhood, Cathba had warned the king it would mean death to him if he saw her. Nevertheless, he often heard of Darthool from Lavarcam, who in her going to and fro had ever one thing to say—that never had there been any woman so beautiful.

The rumour of this great loveliness spread from lip to lip. Yet no man ventured to seek out the hidden place where Darthool dwelled, for to all it was known that Concobar kept her there against the time when he would make her his queen, and all feared the long arm and the heavy hand of Concobar Mac Nessa. None might even question the king.

It was in this year that the shadows of the feet of Fate came into that place.

One day when Lavarcam told the king that Darthool grew fairer and fairer, so that even the wild creatures of the forest rejoiced in her, he all but yielded to his desire. Nevertheless, fearing the prophetic voice, he refrained, but cried : " When the snow time has passed, and the first greening is over, and the wild rose runs like a flame throughout the land, then will I go to Darthool."

But before the greening was lost in the tides of summer, and before the wild rose had begun to run like a windy flame throughout the land, Concobar had learned that Destiny waits on no man.

One dawn the first snows came over the hills of the north and fell upon the forest. At the rising of the sun they ceased, but every branch was a white plume, and every glade was smooth and white as was the breast of Darthool herself. There was no wind in the deep blue sky, but the air was sharp and sweet because of the frost. For joy Darthool clapped her hands, as she stood upon the wall of the lios.

Then, glancing downward, she beheld the woman who was her attendant standing beside a calf that had been slain for the provisioning of those within the fort. The red blood streamed over the snow, and was as the crimson cloak of an Ultonian chief there, till the red grew mottled as it sank through the frozen whiteness.

Darthool's eyes ever saddened at the sight of blood, but after a brief while she knew that there was no harm in that shedding, and that no omen of further bloodspilling lay therein.

While she was still looking thereon, a great raven, glossy black and burnished in the sun rays, came gliding swift across the snow, and alit by the slain calf, and drank of the warm bright blood.

Of a sudden Darthool laughed low.   It was a sweet shy laugh, and Lavarcam, who had come to her side, asked her why there was such sweet low laughter upon her.   Mayhap she knew; mayhap she guessed that Darthool dreamed dreams of love, because her womanhood was now come, and because of the old heroic tales she took so great a pleasure in, and because of the vision that every woman has in her heart.

"I was thinking, Lavarcam," she said.

"And what was that thought, Darthool?"

"It was this: that if there be anywhere a youth whose skin is white as that whiteness there, and whose locks are as dark and glossy as the plumage of that raven, and in whose cheek is a crimson as red as that blood that is upon the snow, then of a surety him could I love, and that gladly."

For a moment Lavarcam said nought; then the power of Destiny moved her.

"There is one man who is more beautiful

than all others I have ever seen.  He is young, and his hair is dark and glossy as that raven's wing, and in his cheek the ruddy flame is as that crimson blood, and his skin is as white as any sunlit whiteness, or as thine own breast, Darthool."

"And what will be the name of that man, Lavarcam, and whence is he and where, and what is his degree?"

"He is called Nathos, and is the son of Usna, who is a great lord in Alba.  But he is now in Emania, among the company of the king; and with him are his brothers, both fair to see, and princes among men because of their beauty and valour, yet neither so surpassing all men as Nathos.  They are called Ailne and Ardan."[1]

That was a fatal saying of Lavarcam, for it sank into the mind of Darthool as moonlight into dark water.

Day by day thereafter she thought of nothing but of meeting this proud son of beauty;

[1] I have adopted here, as more euphonious, the name given to the eldest of the sons of Usna (Uisneach) by Macpherson in "Darthula."  The old spelling is *Naoise.* *Ainnle* (Ailne, Ailthos) means "beautiful," and *Ardan,* "pride."

night by night she dreamed of Nathos and of his love.

At the last, Lavarcam was filled with fear, for she saw that her words had awakened the flaming lion that lies hid in the heart. And truly it was not long till Darthool spoke to her of her longing and deep desire, and how that without Nathos she did not care to live.

For a time Lavarcam smiled ; but when she saw that the king's beautiful ward was ever growing more and more wrought, her heart smote her.

One day, as she was returning from Emain Macha, she met a swineherd, clad roughly in the fell of a deer, and with him were two men, rude, dishevelled hillmen, bondagers to the Ultonians.

These, notwithstanding the law of Concobar, she took with her into the forest, and bade them await at a well that was there, until they heard the cry of a jay and the bark of a hill-fox, when they were to move slowly on their way, but to speak to no one whom they might meet, and above all to be silent after they left the shadow of the wood.

Having done this, she entered the lios, and

asked Darthool to come forth with her into the woods.

When they drew near to the well, Lavarcam moved aside to look for some rare herb, as she said. Soon the cry of the jay and the bark of the hill-fox were in the air.

"That is a strange thing," Darthool said to her, when she was by her side again ; "for that cry of the jay was the cry it gives in April, at the nesting time, and the bark of that hill-fox was the bark it gives in the season of the rut, many months agone."

"Hush," said Lavarcam, "and look."

They stood still, as they saw the swineherd and the two hillmen rise from near the well, and move slowly across the glade.

"Who are these, Lavarcam?" asked Darthool, with wonder in her eyes.

"These are men, daughter of Felim."

"They are younger than those I have seen from the outskirts of the forest, but they are wild in dress and mien, and are not of high degree, and my eyes have no pleasure in looking upon them."

"Nevertheless," answered Lavarcam, " these are the three sons of Usna—Nathos and Ailne and Ardan."

For a brief while Darthool looked upon them.  Then she spoke.

"The truth flew past thy lips, Lavarcam. Yonder man whom ye name Nathos has neither raven hair nor white skin, nor the comely red in his face ; and the two others are like the slaves I saw that day I beheld the foster-brothers of Concobar driving back from battle, in a chariot dragged by wild rough men in bondage.  I remember the day, for it was then that thou bade me know that death was the portion of any man who sought me.  That, too, I fear was no true word.  Howsoever, as to these men, they may go.  And yet—— wait."

And with that Darthool moved swiftly forward, and, coming upon the three men by a by-path through the fern, confronted them.

They stood amazed at her exceeding great beauty.  Nothing like it was in the whole world ; so, little wonder that these boors stood as though the face of death was bare to them ; for beauty is strange and terrible to most men, and they are prone to stand in dread of it.

None spake.  Darthool looked at each, a slow smile of mocking in her lips, a blue flame of scorn in her eyes.

" Are ye the sons of Usna?"

They made no answer, but stared unwaveringly upon her, as do the dull cattle in the fields.

"What brave courtesy!" she cried, mocking with her sweet voice, "how swift in courtesy! Tell me, Nathos, son of Usna, is it the wont of thy people in Alba to stand by agape when a woman speaks? Who is Usna, or what? If he is a king, is he overlord of swineherds? If it is a place, is it the rough bogs of the hills where sword-clad men do not go, but only a poor folk clad rudely in skins?"

Still they answered nothing.

"Were ye whipt into silence when ye were young, ye that stand there wordless as dogs? If indeed ye be the sons of Usna, then truly Concobar MacNessa must be in sore want of men at Emain Macha!"

At that the swineherd could no longer hold to his bond.

"By thy great exceeding beauty I know that thou art no other than Darthool, whom the king hides in this place. But do not mock us, who would rather worship thee. We are no nobles, but a swineherd, and two hillmen who are bondagers to Cairbre of the Three Duns."

At that Darthool laughed gently.

" That I knew full well, swineherd, for all that I dwell here apart and see none of my kind, save Maev my nurse and Aeifa my tutor and Lavarcam the friend of the king. Those I have seen otherwise have been beheld a great way off, from where I laid hid in the woods. But now, wilt thou do one thing for me ? "

" I will give thee my life."

Darthool smiled into the man's eyes, and what was only the swineherd died, and a strong heroic soul arose in him.

" I would fain see Nathos, the eldest of the sons of Usna."

" That is against the law of Concobar : and long is the arm and heavy the hand of Concobar MacNessa the high king. But what is death to me, since thou willest me to do this thing for thee, Darthool of the beautiful eyes ? Nay, I swear this thing : that rather would I die by torture, and please thee, than live out my life and refuse thee of what thou art fain. For thy beauty is upon me like the light of the moon at the full on the dark moorland. I am thine."

Darthool looked at the man. Suddenly she stooped and kissed him on the wind-furrowed brow. Great fortune was his, and he was well repaid for his death by blunt spear-shafts, when Concobar knew all. For what is death, when a man has reached beyond the limit of his desire ?

"Then go this night to Nathos, and tell him that I, Darthool, dream of him by day and by night, and that if he is in anywise fain of me, let him come to me to-morrow, an hour before the setting of the sun, at this well."

With that she turned and walked slowly back to where Lavarcam awaited her. As they moved homeward through the wood, Lavarcam saw that the dream in the eyes of Darthool had deepened. It was in vain then, or later, that she sought to know what the fair, beautiful girl had said to the swineherd. She feared, however, that Darthool no longer trusted her because of the lie that she had told, and that mayhap the girl had plotted somewhat with the swineherd.

All the morrow Lavarcam watched Darthool closely, but she seemed rapt in vision, and cared neither to chase the fawns, nor to fish, nor even to wander idly through the woods. No speech would she have with any one, and said only that she wished to lie under the boughs of the great oak in front of the lios, and sleep.

" How can that be, when there is snow upon the ground ? " Lavarcam asked.

" Is there snow upon the ground ? " answered Darthool dreamily. " Then I will lie upon my deerskins, and Aeifa can play to me and sing me songs till dusk."

Hearing that, Lavarcam was glad, for now she could leave the lios with a mind at rest.

So, in the wane of the day, she passed through the forest and came out upon the great plain in front of Emain Macha, and went to seek the king to take counsel with him.

Nevertheless, Lavarcam was sore wrought by Darthool, and would fain have given her her heart's desire. Piteous indeed had her plaints been. With tears and reproaches and sweet beseechings nigh intolerable, Darthool had begged her to bring Nathos to her, if for once only, so that she might at least see him, and know what her heart's desire was like. Moreover, was it not a bitter thing for her to be kept there in that lonely place, and neither to see nor converse with her own kind, and to be kept away from all the joys of youth, and to pass from spring to summer, and from summer

to autumn, and from autumn to winter, yea and
from year to year, and be exiled there, to hear
no young voices, no young laughter?  When
she pleaded thus, Lavarcam was sorrowful
indeed, for she had the heart of a woman, and
knew the beauty and the wonder and the
mystery of love.

Thinking of these things, her heart smote her
as she fared towards Emain Macha, and at the
last she decided to say no word to the king as
to what she feared Darthool may have told the
swineherd.  Furthermore, she muttered, what
was death to her who had known all that life
had to give her?  At the worst, Concobar
could put death upon her.  Had she not lived
and known love, and now was weary?

When she drew nigh to Emain Macha she
saw three ravens and three hoodie-crows and
three kites arise from some carrion hidden in
the long grass that waved there.

When she came upon it, she saw that it was
the body of the swineherd, loose with the
gaping wounds of blunt spear-shafts.  In thus-
wise she knew that Concobar had in some way
heard of what the man had done.

Yet she had no fear from that.  The swineherd was still now.  Neither king nor raven,

neither man nor hoodie-crow, neither spear-shaft nor kite could now hurt him. It was better to be alive than to be dead, but it was well to be dead.

So Lavarcam turned, and went over to the camp in Emain Macha where the sons of Usna were. There she saw Nathos, and told him privily that Darthool longed to see him, and that the forest was open to the stealthy flight of the owl as well as to the soaring hawk.

Nathos was indeed fair to see, and looking upon him Lavarcam knew in her heart that Darthool would love him, and he her. He listened, and she saw his eyes deepen, and a flush come and go upon his face. For sure there was a beating swift of his pulse in that hour.

Nevertheless, he could not come straightway, for Concobar knew that the swineherd had spoken to him of Darthool, and it was for this, and having seen and spoken with the girl, that the king had put the man to death—though for that, added Nathos, little did the swineherd care, for he died laughing and mocking, and, when he lay still, there was a smile upon his face.

" And that was because Darthool had looked into his eyes, Nathos, son of Usna."

"Truly, he died well. I know a prince among men who also would die gladly if Darthool would look into his eyes with love."

" Then come soon and hunt the deer in the solitudes to the north of the forest : and there, amid the woods, or in some glen, or on the hill-slopes, surely thou shalt meet with Darthool —and yet none know of it."

So Lavarcam and Nathos made a bond between them, and parted.

Thereafter days passed. On the morrow of the seventh day Darthool was wandering among the glades and thickets of the uplands far away from the lios, rejoicing in her new freedom and hoping that one day her eyes might look upon Nathos. She was dreaming her dream, when she started at a strange sound, the like of which she had never heard.

That far-off baying of hounds she knew, for oftentimes of old Concobar had ridden to the forest with his deerhounds : but that strange, wild, blazoning sound—— Was it the voice of the flying creature the hounds pursued ?

Then the thought came to her that it was the hunting horn she had often heard of in the songs and war-ballads which Lavarcam and Aeifa were wont to sing to her.

But after that blast the horn no more tore the silence of the deep woods, and the hounds were still: for Nathos had left the chase of the deer and was now moving listless through the green glooms of the forest. Night and day since Lavarcam and the swineherd had told him of Darthool he had dreamed of the beautiful daughter of Felim the Harper. Remembering the last chant of Cathba the Druid, he recalled how Darthool had been named the Beauty of the World, and because he was himself a poet and a dreamer the vision had become part of his life, so that neither by night nor by day was there any hour wherein he did not see in his mind the tall, white-robed figure of Darthool, and the beauty of her eyes, and her face as the sweet wild face of a dream.

And so dreaming he stood at the edge of a glade, his swift eyes watching a fawn dispart a thicket that was close by. Yet it was no fawn as he thought: but rather was it as though a sudden flood of sunshine burst forth in that place. For a woman came from the thicket more beautiful than any dream he had ever dreamed. She was clad in a saffron robe over white that was like the shining of the sun on foam of the sea, and this was claspt with great bands of yellow gold, and over her shoulders was the golden rippling flood of her hair, the sprays of which lightened into delicate fire, and made a mist before him, in the which he could see her eyes like two blue pools wherein purple shadows dreamed.

So exceeding great was her beauty that Nathos did not think of her as Darthool or as any mortal woman, but rather as a daughter of the elder gods, or of that bright divine race of the Tuatha-De-Danann, whose beauty surpassed that of human beings as the beauty of the primrose bank that of the brown sod. He looked upon her amazed, and in a silent worship. If she were indeed of the Dedannan folk, she might disappear at any moment as a shadow goes, that now is here asleep upon the grass and in the twinkling of an eye is among the things of oblivion.

At last speech rose to his lips.

" O fair and wonderful one, whom I see well art of the old sacred race of the Tuatha-De-Danann, may I have word with thee ? It may well be that thou art no other than the wife of Midir himself, she who lives in a fair shining grianan in the hollow of a hill, and lives upon the beauty and fragrance of flowers." Darthool looked at him, and her heart beat. He was in truth fair to see : fairer even than him whom she had imaged in her dreams, or him of whom Lavarcam had spoken.

"Speak. What wouldst thou ? "

" I am faring idly through this lonely land, and I know not where I am. Yonder, in the valley behind the oak-glade, is a high-walled rath. Is it a place of the Shee, and so forbidden ? or who dwells there, and shall a spear or welcome greet me if I enter ? "

" Indeed, thou mayst enter there, and a welcome awaits thee, O Nathos, son of Usna."

" Thou knowest my name, O fair one ; then, indeed, thou art of the old wondrous race, who know swifter than our thought, and whose sight is further and deeper than our sight."

" I am no queen, Nathos, nor am I of the Tuatha-De-Danann, but am a woman as other women are. If I am beautiful in thine eyes, of that I am right glad, for thou art fairer to me than any man I have seen or dreamed of, and my pulse leaps when thine eyes look into mine. I am Darthool, the daughter of Felim the Harper ; yet am I no better than a slave, for

here am I bound to stay, and see no one save
Lavarcam and my two women, and here I shall
die for loneliness and longing."

Nathos heard her sweet low voice with delight, and it was with joy at his heart he knew
she was no strange Dedannan but a woman
of his own race, and that she was Darthool.
Love rose suddenly within him like a flame:
a red flame was it that was in his heart, and a
white flame in his mind, and out of these two
flames is wrought the love of love and the
passion of passion and the dream of dreams.

"Art thou, indeed, Darthool?" he whispered;
"art thou that Darthool of whom I have
dreamed? Strange is the strangeness of this
meeting, O white daughter of Felim. For so
great is thy beauty that I was fain to believe I
saw before me one of the queens of the Tuatha-
De-Danann. But is this thing true, that against
thine own will Concobar the high king keeps
thee here like a trapped bird among these
woods?"

"True it is, and more: for it is not even
by Concobar's will that I roam the woodlands. He was fain that I should never leave
the rath save with Lavarcam, and that I should
spend most of my days within the stone walls

of the dreary lios where he has doomed me to dwell."

"Darthool, my heart is filled with a rising tide. That tide is love. Thou hast not seen the sea : but there, when the tide flows, there is nothing, there is no one, in all the world, which can say it nay. So is my love for thee, that now rises ; and, once thine, will be thine evermore. Yet I would not put this upon thee ; and if thy words and looks come out of thy frank, sweet courtesy and open maidenly heart, and mean no more than that thou carest for me as a brother, it is thy brother I will be, Darthool, to serve thee and succour thee and love thee evermore, and in that way only."

For a brief while she looked at him. Then the noon-blue of her eyes deepened, and a flush drifted through her face and waned into the deeper red of her parted lips.

"Nathos," she said in a low voice, which trembled as a reed in the wind, " I, too, love. It is thee I love. If it be wrong for me, a maiden, to speak thus, forgive me, for I have grown wilding here, and am more akin to the fawns of the forest than to womenkind of mine own age or estate. But I love thee, Nathos : as of old, in the far-off Dedannan days, Dectura the queen loved the Green Harper, and went forth with him and was seen no more of her own people."

" If thou indeed wilt have it so, Darthool, be thou my Dectura, and let me be thy Green Harper. For beyond the reach of life or death is the greatness of the love I feel for thee, even now in this first hour of our meeting."

" Thy words are in my heart, Nathos ; and because that this is so, I now put *geas* upon thee. Let thy sword be as my sword, and be thou to me as brother and friend and the holder of my leal love ; and to this end, lo ! I throw this yellow thistle against thy cheek, to raise a mark of shame there if thou dost not fulfil the bond, and there to be seen of all men as a sign and witness of thy disgrace ; yea, even thus I put *geas* upon thee, to succour me in my ill fate, to take me unto thyself, to give thyself unto me, and to let us go forth together heedless of Fate."

Nathos looked at her with proud eyes.

" Of a surety, Darthool, there is no hero of the Red Branch who hath a courage greater than thine, even though it may be that thou speakest the more freely from knowing little of what may befall."

"What can befall save death, and dost thou fear death, son of Usna?"

Nathos smiled out of grave eyes.

"If I feared death, Darthool, I would not now be speaking with thee here. It is swift silence upon any who in this forbidden land speaks with the daughter of Felim the Harper. Concobar MacNessa has the ears of a hare and the eyes of a hawk and the swoop of an eagle. Dost thou remember the swineherd to whom thou gavest word privily? Well, that night he lay in the grass tended only by the raven and the wolf, for he was done to death with blunt spear-shafts."

"For that I have deep grief," said Darthool, with tears drifting like a rainy mist athwart the blue of her eyes.

"Nevertheless, he died with a smile, Darthool. Thou hadst looked into his eyes and kissed him. Even so, and for less now, would I too die."

"That thou shalt not do, Nathos;" and even as she spoke Darthool moved forward and put her honeysweet lips against the mouth of Nathos, and made his blood leap, and a flame come into his eyes, and a trembling come into his limbs.

Then, as though with that kiss she had become as a wild rose, she stood swaying lightly, her fair face delicately aflame. Nathos put his arms about her, and kissed her on the brow and on the lips.

"That kiss on the brow is for service," he said, "because from this hour thou art my queen ; and that kiss on the lips is for love, for from this hour I shall love no woman save thee thyself, but shall be thine and thine only in life or death."

Nevertheless, though Nathos accepted the *geas* put upon him by Darthool, he was troubled at the thought of the anger of Concobar the high king. It would be a swift and bitter death for him, and for Darthool too it might be death or worse.

The thought in his mind swam into his eyes, and Darthool saw it. She shrank from him, and stood hesitating and as though about to flee at his first word of doubt. When he looked at her again his last fear went.

" Fair wonderful one, thou art as a fawn there in the fern where thou standest ; Darthool, do not doubt the truth of my words. I am thine to love and to serve, and am under *geas* to thee. But my thought was this : if

we two go hence and are waylaid, it will be
death, and if we go hence and are not waylaid
forthwith, it will still be death; for long is the
arm, and heavy the hand, and tireless the quest
of Concobar MacNessa. And this, too: that
if we cross the Moyle and go to Alba, it may
still be death; yea, though for a year or for a
brood of years we elude the undying wrath and
vengeance of the king."

" He will forget when once the bird is flown.
Neither the bird nor the wind leaves any track,
so let our flight be as that of the bird and our
way be as that of the wind."

" The king forgetteth not. If so be that we
might escape him many years, he will yet have
his will of us in the end; and this though thou
wert old, Darthool, and wert no longer his
desire, and though I were outlawed and broken
and no more in his sight than a wolf of the
hills, good to slay if come upon, but not worthy
of chase."

" Concobar is not a king in Alba ?"

" No."

" Then let us go to thine own land. He
can do no more than send emissaries after
us, and with these thou canst deal swiftly,
Nathos."

At that, Nathos lightly laughed.

"Truly, I am seeing Concobar as a man sees his own shadow in the water. He is a great king in Uladh, but he is no more in Alba than any hero of the Red Branch. Come, Darthool; across the Moyle are the pine-green shores of Alba. It is a fair, beautiful land. The sea-lochs reach far among pine-clad hills, and green pastures are on the slopes of the great mountains and around the shadowy, inland waters. The forests are full of deer and wild birds, the rivers and lochs of fish, the pastures of cattle and sheep and swift brown mares. Thou shalt have milk to drink, and the red flesh of the salmon, and the brown flesh of the deer, and the white flesh of the badger. Thou shalt lack for nothing, who art my queen; and thou shalt have love till the sun grows a lordlier fire and the stars leap in their slow dance from dusk to dawn."

"I will come," Darthool whispered, with glad eyes.

"Only thou must not delay. Thy coming must be now. Thou must not even enter the rath again. Otherwise it is never the waters of the Moyle that we shall see, but only the red flame in the eyes of Concobar."

Even while Nathos spoke his eyes grew hard, and his hands slipped to the javelin he had by his side. While Darthool watched him in amaze, he swung the iron-pointed shaft at a place where a bent bracken hung listless in the air.

"Is it a wolf?" cried Darthool, in sudden affright.

"It is worse than a wolf," answered Nathos; "for if thou wilt go to that place thou wilt see either a slain man, or the form of a man, in the grass beneath the bracken."

Swiftly Darthool ran to the spot wherein the javelin had swung singing. There was no one there, but, where the javelin still quivered slightly, she saw the still warm shape of a crouching man, and discerned, by the bending of the bracken, what course he must have twisted away.

Nathos followed and stood beside her. As he stooped to pluck the javelin from the ground, he descried a wooden-hilted knife.

"It is as I thought," he said gravely. "Concobar has set a spy upon me. No Ultonian carries a knife such as this. It belongs to the hillmen of the north-west, of whom a few years agone we made slaves. Mayhap

one of these men who were with the swineherd
has been told to follow me secretly whereso-
ever I go."

Darthool turned and looked at Nathos with
eyes filled with a new fear, because of her love
of him.

He took her hand in his.

"There is yet time, Darthool. Wilt thou
go back to the rath, and stay there till Concobar wills thee to be his wife?"

"I cannot go back."

"Then come, O Darthool."

And with that the twain turned and moved
swiftly northward through the forest, by the
way Nathos had already passed.

"By dawn we may reach the dun where my
two brothers now are, and for that day and
that night we may rest in safety," whispered
Nathos, as Darthool turned and looked for the
last time upon the place where she had lived
all these years.

"But thereafter, O love that I have won,
the wind must be in our hair and the dead
leaves be upon the soles of our feet, for there
can be no resting for us till we are away from
this land: no, and not for us only, but also
for Ailne and Ardan. Concobar will not rest

content with bitter wrath, and, if he cannot track the stag, will slay the fawns."

Soon thereafter they drew near the place where Nathos had left his hounds and his huntsmen. Bidding Darthool hide among the bracken and undergrowth, he went forward alone and told the men to go back to the dun of the sons of Usna, but not till the third day, and by circuitous ways. Thus he hoped that he might the longer elude Concobar, whose emissaries would follow the track of his hounds.

Thereafter Nathos and Darthool fared swiftly hand in hand through the sombre ways of the forest. While it was still light they emerged upon a great moor, which they crossed, and then ascended the gorges of the hills. There the night fell, as though a wind-drifted darkness suddenly suspended and then swiftly enshrouded everything. They dreaded to rest, and yet so deep was the darkness that they could fare no farther.

But while they were still whispering the one to the other, Darthool descried a soft, silver shining, like a dewy gossamer. It was the little group of seven stars that we call the Pleiades.

"See," she whispered, "An Grioglachan! When they shine, others will soon be seen." And so it was.

All through the night the fugitives hastened onward by the light of the stars, ever keeping close to each other, for the mountain solitudes were full of dreadful noises, and in the black tarns among the peaty moss they could hear the moaning of the kelpie, or on the shores of the hill-lochs the shrill neighing of the water-horses, terrible creatures of the darkness.

For the last hour of the dark they rested a brief while, lying close hid among the bracken, in a sheltered place on a rocky mountain slope. Darthool heeded little now the weariness and fears of that perilous faring by night, for she was with Nathos; and Nathos now was glad, and no longer cared whether death was sure or not. He fell asleep there under the morning stars, among the winter-brown bracken, with Darthool's head upon his breast; and his last thought was, that if the swineherd had died smiling because Darthool's eyes had looked into his, how well might he too die content if his hour came suddenly upon him.

The dawn wavered among the hills, but still they slept.

A wolf tracking a wounded doe howled, and the howling wailed from corrie to corrie. Darthool stirred, but slept again. An eagle screamed as it rose and wheeled against the broadening light, but its wild voice was drowned in silence. Then came the first sun-rays rippling, dancing, leaping, from amid the crested heights and peaks to the eastward, and Nathos awoke.

For some moments he lay breathless with wonder. Darthool, in all her radiant beauty, was by his side, her golden hair ablaze in the sunlight, and her fair face like a flower amid the bracken. It was too great a wonder. Then he knew that Concobar's hounds might any hour now be upon them, and so he put his dream away from him, and stooped and kissed Darthool upon the lips. With a cry she woke, and put her arms about him. Hard it was for him to add to her weariness; but she rose at once, and seemed, indeed, in his eyes, as fresh as any fawn of the hill-side. She went to a little tarn close by and drank of the cool, sweet water.

As she drank Nathos looked at her, and again wondered if she were not one of the divine race of old, the mysterious Tuatha-De-

Danann, whom, ages before, the Milesians had driven to the hills and remote places. So fair was she that his heart ached. Then a swift pulse of joy leaped within him, and he was glad with a great gladness.

Thereafter they sped swiftly onward, and now Nathos exulted, for he recognised the peaks and the trend of the valleys. Within an hour from the rising of the sun he saw the grey walls of the dun of the sons of Usna.

His long cry—that of the heron thrice repeated—brought Ailne and Ardan forth. Darthool looked at them wondering, for they, too, were taller and nobler than other men, and only less beautiful in her eyes than Nathos himself.

But if she wondered, much more did they marvel at what they saw. Never had they beheld any woman so beautiful, and their first thought was that of Nathos, that Darthool was of the fair divine race who were now so seldom seen of men.

But when Nathos had told them all, and that she who was now his bride was no other than that Darthool whom Concobar the high king had set aside to become his queen, they were filled with sorrow. Well they knew that

Concobar MacNessa would not lightly relin-
quish the fair maid whom he had so long
secreted in the forest-lios, and that blood would
flow because of this thing.

"Moreover," said Ailne, "hast thou forgotten the prophecy? There is the saying of
Cathba the Druid, of which we have all heard:
that from the daughter of Felim the Harper
would come sorrow to the king, and severance
of the Red Branch from the lost kingdom of
Uladh, and rivers of blood."

"That may be, Ailne, my brother," Nathos
answered; "but I ask none to go with me
into this doom, if that doom indeed must be,
though mayhap the dark hour of it is passed.
For Darthool and I shall now fare forward,
with some of our following, and with horses
and food, and haply we may reach the coast
and find our great galley in the Creek of the
Willows, where we secreted it, and so gain the
shores of Alba before Concobar can overtake
us."

But while Ailne pondered, Ardan spoke.

"That shall not be, Nathos. Listen! By
the Sun and the Wind I swear that where
thou goest I will go, and that I will never
desert thee nor Darthool, who is now our

sister. If the doom must come, let it come. What is death, that it should put a paleness into the face of love? Are we not close-kin, children of one mother, and is not Darthool thy wife now and our sister, and are we not henceforth as one? Speak, Ailne, is it not so?"

"It is so. Ardan has spoken for me. But I say nothing, for I feel upon us the shadow of that doom of which, as we have heard, Cathba the Druid spoke."

But here Darthool moved forward.

"Listen, Nathos, and ye, Ailne and Ardan, my brothers: it is not for me to bring sorrow upon the king and upon the Red Branch and upon Uladh, and still less upon ye, my brothers, and upon thee, Nathos. Therefore, let me now go back to the lios, and tell Lavarcam, who will tell the king, that I have no will to stray, and that I will abide in that place till I die, or till Concobar dare put his face against Fate and take me thence."

At that Nathos smiled only. There was no word to say; in his eyes was all his answer to Darthool.

But Ardan answered for himself and Ailne:

"Though the stars fall, beautiful daughter

of Felim, who art now Darthool, our sister, we shall not leave thee, nor suffer thee to go from us save by thine own free will, and that in no fear for what may befall us. Nathos and Ailne and Ardan are the three sons of Usna, upon whom long ago *geas* was set, that each would abide by each until death."

Thereupon all kissed each other, and took the deep vow of fealty. The sons of Usna knew well that it would be a madness to withstand Concobar in their dun, strong as it was ; for in time he would take the place, as dogs hunt out the badger from its lair, and at the best would still starve them into surrender or death.

So with all speed they summoned those of their following who were under the sword-bond, and put together food and raiment, and then mounted and rode swiftly away.

As they passed the highest ridge to the eastward that night they looked back. A red light flared in a valley far to the west. It was their dun, a torch amid the darkness. A single column of flame rose above it, and wavered to and fro. And by that sign they knew that the long arm and the heavy hand of Concobar MacNessa had already reached out towards them. Three times fifty men went with them, and so swift was their flight and so sure their way that before long they came to the coast-lands. There, in the Creek of the Willows, the long black galley was found; and swiftly all embarked.

It was with glad eyes that Darthool and the sons of Usna saw the dancing waves of the sea, and felt its free breath break upon them. From three great tiers, fifty score men to each, the vassals thrust out their long oars, and with their blades threshed the waters into a yeast of foam. In the dazzle of the sea Darthool rejoiced, and made the hearts of all there to swell because of an exceeding sweet song she sang.

Nathos and Ailne and Ardan sat beside her, and could scarce take from her face their dreaming eyes.

Towards noon the wind shifted, and slid out of the north towards the west. Then the great sail was hoisted, and bellied out to the steady breeze, and the oars were shipped. The black galley now flew along the waters like a cormorant. Darthool laughed with joy at this new beautiful world of the sea, and never tired of trailing her hands in the swift lapsing wave, or in the send of the following billow.

In the afternoon they came close to the shores of Alba, and made northward, past many isles and through narrow straits and fjords. In one and all Darthool took pleasure, and was glad indeed that the land of Nathos was so beautiful.

At sundown they reached the eastern shores of the great island of Mull, and there the wind failed them, so the galley was put into a bay that is now the bay of Aros.

There the sons of Usna debated long as to what course to follow. Nathos and Ailne thought it best to move inland, and to gain the protection of the high king of Alba; but Darthool feared this because of a dream she had thrice dreamed, wherein she saw a strange king and a strange folk laughing over the slain body of Nathos, while she stood by crowned but a captive. As for Ardan, he said only that the sons of Usna should go to where their father's dun had been, before the last king of Alba had destroyed it.

That night a galley came to them from the long island of Lismore. In it were a score of men, commanded by a lord of Appin, named

Fergus of the Three Duns. With him was a stranger, clad in a rich robe of fur, so claspt across the throat with gold that the hood he wore fell about and covered his face. While Fergus spake with the sons of Usna, and told them how they had been seen by men of his in a swift war-galley, off the south coast of Mull, and urged them also to go inland to meet the king, the stranger looked steadfastly upon Darthool.

When at last he had to speak to the brothers he addressed them courteously, but in a Gaelic strange to their ears. He bade them come with him to his high-walled dun, a brief way inland : to come alone, as his guests, and to bring Darthool with them.

"It is not well to go to a man's dun, and not be knowing that man's name," said Nathos courteously.

The stranger hesitated, and looked at Fergus.

"They call me Angus Mudartach," he said. But at that Darthool asked him to let her look upon his face.

"For it is not meet," she added, "that we should go to a man's dun and not have seen his face."

Angus of Moidart drew back his hood.

Darthool's lips grew pale. Then she smiled.

"Let us rest here for to-night, Angus Mudartach," she said, "and, if thou wilt come again on the morrow after to-morrow, thou canst take us with thee to thy great dun. But meanwhile we have travelled far and swiftly, and would fain rest: and, as thou seest, the skies are clear, and we want for nothing."

Once more Angus pleaded to the sons of Usna.

"Ye are brave men, and can laugh at weariness or danger. But if the island be swept by a great storm to-night, or if the followers of Concobar, king of the northlands of Erin, come upon ye, or if other misadventure befall, shall ye wantonly expose this fair young princess? Nay, rather, let her come with me, and she shall not only be safe in my great rath of Dunchraig, but there my wife and her maidens shall make much of her, and give her white robes and golden torques and garments of delicate furs. This maid whom ye call Darthool is too young to be thrown thus idly before the feet of the evil powers who are for ever clamouring for death."

But, at a sign from Darthool, Nathos refused ; saying, with gracious words and courteous mien, that it would rejoice them all to visit Angus Mudartach later, but not then.

So Angus of Moidart turned, frowning, and went back to his galley with Fergus of the Three Duns.   And as he went he asked mutteringly how many men the sons of Usna had with them.   When he learned that there were thrice fifty, and that Fergus had but a score and ten men with him, he said no more.

When the strangers had gone, Nathos turned to Darthool and asked why she had not shown more graciousness to one who was surely a great lord among the Alban Gaels, and why she would not go with him.

"Because, Nathos, that man who called himself Angus Mudartach is no other than the King of Alba.   He it is whom I saw in my dreams, laughing over your slain body, and beside whom I stood crowned and yet a captive.   And by that token I warn ye of this thing : that the Alban king desireth me, and would fain slay ye all, or deliver ye into the hands of Concobar MacNessa."

Nathos stood brooding, but Ardan stepped forward.

" Darthool is right.   And wise she was, too, to bid this Angus of Moidart come on the morrow after to-morrow.   Nevertheless, I know well by hearsay of his vassal, Fergus of the Three Duns, and that the man is called Fergus the Wily.   He will not wait, but at dawn will be about us, with thrice fifty and thrice fifty again."

"Ardan has spoken well," added Nathos. " There is but one thing to be done.   Weary we are, but we must go hence at once."

And so it was.   The dusk was heavy upon sea and land that night, and a sea-mist came up and obscured the skies, so that not a star was visible.

Soundlessly they launched the great galley again, and once more set sail.   The night-wind was from the south-east, whereat they rejoiced, for thus there was no need of the oars, and so no betraying thresh would be heard.

When they were well north of Lismore they put out the long oars and swung the galley northwards.   It was with relief that the sons of Usna passed the Appin lands, and before dawn rowed into a great sea-loch.

There, however, they learned that the King

of Alba, he who had called himself Angus Mudartach, was in the westlands only for a brief while, and would have to haste to Dunedin straightway, as runners had come with tidings of a great rising. He had no rath of Dunchraig, and no dun there; and so in truth the sons of Usna knew that the king had lied to them, and that Darthool was right. As for Fergus of the Three Duns, he was no longer a great lord, but had been despoiled, and at the most could summon two score and ten men.

So the sons of Usna greatly rejoiced, for now they could go to their own land in safety, which lay beyond the region held by Fergus of the Duns.

For seven days they stayed by the shores of that sea-loch, under the shadow of mighty mountains. Ardan, with a scanty following, went through the hill-passes, and returned saying that the King of Alba had gone to his own country and that all the great lords of the region had departed with him, including Fergus.

So on the eighth day the galley sailed a short way southward once more, and entered into the Bay of Selma. There, on a rocky eminence, were the walls of their great dun, which Usna their father had built among the ruins of the chief stronghold of the Cruithne, the ancient people of Alba.[1]

It was with joy that the sons of Usna saw once more the house of their childhood, and with still greater joy that they found the people of the neighbouring glens and straths still loyal to them. Their father Usna had ever been at war with the King of Alba, and after many battles (the bards sang of the beauty of Usna's wife as the torch that lit those wars) he had conquered all this region. But at his death, by treachery the king had overcome the stronghold and destroyed it.

But now again the sons of Usna had their home in their own eyrie. They knew not how long they might abide there in peace, for either the King of Alba, or Fergus of the Duns as his leader of men, would come again when once peace in the eastlands was secured.

There Nathos wished to dwell alone with Darthool and a few followers, but Ailne and

---

[1] The Cruithne, or Picts, had their chief stronghold at Beregonium, overlooking the Bay of Selma, not far from the mouth of Loch Etive, below the Falls of Lora, in West Argyll.

Ardan once more refused to leave him then or ever. But glad were the thrice fifty vassals to return to their own land, and without regret the sons of Usna saw them set sail for Erin. They were men who cared little for aught save strife, and when not wielding sword or spear were haughty and bitter with all other men save those of the Red Branch, and so were only a danger and a weariness in that place.

Throughout that winter they lived there in peace, hunting and fishing. So great was the love of each for Darthool that every day was full of peace and content wherein they saw her. Nathos moved in a dream, and knew the extreme of joy. At night, before the fire, Darthool sang to them old-world airs of a sweet plaintive music, so sweet and plaintive that men said she must be no other than Fionula, she of the children of Lir who were turned into wild swans, and lived a thousand years in the old, old days.

But when spring came again—a spring so fair and sweet that it was as though May had come hand in hand with February—a rumour reached them that the King of Alba, though he could not penetrate the highlands of the west, intended, with the help of Fergus of the Duns and other chieftains, to proceed once more against the Dun of Usna. Moreover, he had sworn to raze it to the ground, and to slay Nathos, and to take Darthool to be his wife.

Nathos laughed at this, for he knew well that the King of Alba would never take him alive, nor yet Darthool. But after long colloquy with Ailne and Ardan, all decided to set forth and pass northward to the land whence their mother had come, a land of endless mountains and narrow lochs, beautiful beyond any other, grander than any Darthool had seen, and remote beyond the reach of any Alban king.

So thither they set forth, and took with them in their great galley two score and ten men of their own clan. After long sailing up narrow lochs, the sons of Usna reached the mountain land whence their mother had come. Her father was dead, but the great dun he had built upon the summit of one of the hills overlooking the Black Loch had been left unharmed, and was tenanted only by wandering shepherds. Here Nathos and Darthool made their home, and in that beautiful land and in the glory of spring, knew the full joy and richness of life.[1]

For a brief while all the people of the mountain lands round about gave in their adherence to Nathos, so that he became as a king in that region. So great was the fear in which the three sons of Usna were held, and so strong were they in their mountain home, that none dared to approach them with the flaming brand.

Thus three years passed, and in all the wide reaches of the world there was no man so happy as Nathos and no woman so happy as Darthool; and after these there were none so happy as Ailne and Ardan, who were well content to live so that they might be near the beautiful wife of Nathos, their sister, Darthool, fairest of all women in the world.

The King of Alba, whom they had feared, was now dead, and the king who reigned in his place was well disposed towards the sons of Usna and sought their alliance. So this was done, and the name and fame of the three

---

[1] To this day, the Highlander of Western Argyll and of Inverness-shire is familiar with the Fort of the Sons of Usna, above one of the lochs which constitute what is now known as the Caledonian Canal.

brothers spread throughout the land; while from the wild west to the populous east the poets sang of the beauty of Darthool.

In the summer months they abode at the high fort of Darthool, for so they named it, on the heights above the Black Loch, or Loch Ness as we now call it; and from the first frosts till the cuckoo's song had ceased they lived at Dunuisneachan, their father's ancient stronghold by the shores of Loch Etive. Thence often they wandered far afoot, or sailed southward and eastward among the sea-lochs and narrow kyles. They hunted in Glenorchy and fished under the mountain-shadows on Loch Awe; or followed the deer through the woods of Glenlaidhe. When it was pleasant to be upon the waters, they sailed down the long fjord of Loch Fyne, and rested awhile at the Haven of the Foray, and watched the coming and going of the rainbows on the rocky headlands which guard that place; then they would cross to the Cowal, and enter the narrow Kyles of Bute, where on the little isle we call the Burnt Island they built a vitrified fort. Thence they followed past the Hills of Ruel to Glendaruay (Glendaruel), and so to the head of Loch Striven and up Glenmassan, and thence down by the sweet inland waters of Loch Eck, and waterward again by the bay we now call the Holy Loch. Thence up the long, narrow fjord of Loch Long they sailed, till among the mountains they crossed the short pass to Loch Lomond, and perhaps met the soldiery of the King of Alba at the inland lakes, or came upon the great fort of Dumbarton on the Clyde; or they may have crossed the hill to the Gareloch, and so returned westward once more by the blue frith of Clyde, past the precipitous isle of Arran, and so up Loch Fyne again; or seaward by the Mull of Cantire, and thence northward past the isles to their own place, and could once more watch the salmon leaping through the Falls of Lora or chase the deer on the hills of Etive.

But during all this time Concobar, the high king of the Ultonians, nursed his bitter thoughts. He had heard of the great fame and happiness of the sons of Usna, and more than ever he yearned after Darthool, his wrath at his loss being the greater because that all the old prophecies about the beautiful daughter of Felim were unfulfilled.

One day the high king made a great festival in Emain Macha, and never in Erin was seen one more royal and magnificent. The princes and nobles from all the regions in the sway of Concobar were there, and all the musicians, singers, and poets in Uladh.

In the midst of the festival Concobar asked those present at his board if now, in the height of the glory of the Red Branch, they wanted for anything; but they answered as with one voice that they were content.

"And that is what I am not," he answered.

"And wherefore, O king and lord?"

"Because that the three greatest of ye are absent from us. I speak of the three Torches of the Valour of the Gael: Nathos and Ailne and Ardan, the sons of Usna, the son of Congal Claringnech. For now I the king say this: that it is not fitting these three heroes, the pride of our chivalry, should be in exile, and this only because of a woman. By the Sun and Wind, there is no woman alive who is worthy to be the cause of this. Far better were it that the sons of Usna were once more in our midst. Even now they hold half the lands of Alba under the shadow of their sword. Truly they are heroes, and if dark days come upon us, as the soothsayers foretell, then indeed we shall be in sore need of them."

All there were rejoiced at that. There was not one who had not lamented the fierce anger of Concobar, and who was not fain to have the sons of Usna again among the chivalry of the Red Branch. Only fear had not allowed them to speak, for the high king had slain a man who had said that Nathos was too great a lord to be exiled.

"And since ye are so glad at this thing," Concobar added, "and would fain have these heroes among us, to be the chief pride, glory and defence of Uladh against all other kingdoms and provinces of Erin, I say to ye : Go and bring hence again from Alba the three sons of Usna."

"That is well," their spokesman answered ; "but who is to prevail with Nathos and his brothers ? We are willing to go, but we cannot bring Nathos against his will. Moreover, is he not under *geas* not to put foot again in Erin ?"

"Not so. I know that Nathos is under *geas* not to return to Erin unless it be in the company of Fergus, the son of Lossa the Red, or Conall Cernach, or Cuchulain. And look you, each of these is now here, so that I shall well know who most loves me."

So, when the feast was over, Concobar first drew Conall Cernach aside.

"Tell me, O warrior lord," he said, "what wouldst thou say or do if I should send thee for the sons of Usna, and that at my secret command they should be slain privily—a thing, nevertheless, Conall, which I do not purpose to do."

"That could not be done, O king and lord, without a bitter and wrongful bloodshedding, for I could not do otherwise than put death upon each and all of the Ultonians who might be with me on that day."

"That may be so, Conall Cernach. So now, go."

Thereafter the king sent for Cuchulain. The young champion came to him fearlessly, for the whole heart of the warrior prince was noble and courageous.

Concobar asked him the same question as he had asked Conall Cernach.

"What would I do, O lord and king?" answered Cuchulain with proud disdain. "This thing I would do, and my troth to it: that if thou through me brought about the death of the sons of Usna, thou mightst flee eastward to Innia Iarrtharaigh[1] itself, and yet not be safe from perishing by my hand because of thy deed."

Concobar smiled grimly.

"I knew well, Cuchulain, that ye bore me no love," he said; and bade the hero be-gone.

Thereafter the king sent for Fergus, the son of Rossa, and to him he put the same question as to Conall Cernach and to Cuchu-lain.

"This much I say," said Fergus, "that never would I raise hand or weapon against thee: nevertheless, there is not one Ultonian who might fare forth on that errand who would not get the shortness of life and sorrow of death from me."

"It is thou, Fergus, son of Rossa, who dost truly love thy king. It is to thee I entrust this thing, who shalt be greater in Erin than any son of Usna. Go forth on the morrow, and remember thy name of old—Fergus Honeymouth. Of a surety Nathos, with Darthool, and Ailne and Ardan, shall come from Alba with thee. When thou art again

---

[1] Western India.

in Erin, go at once to the house of Borrach, the son of Cainte; and when thou art there stay, because of one of thy *geasa* never to refuse a feast, and beforehand I shall warn Borrach of this thing. Then send forward at once, and without covenant, and without protection, to Emain Macha, the three sons of Usna."

So on the morrow Fergus went forth, taking none with him save his two sons, Illann the Fair, and Buine of the Red Locks, and a man Cullen to steer the sea-barge wherewith he would set sail.

It was a fair voyage, and soon the black barge of Fergus sailed past the isles and headlands of Alba, and came to Loch Etive and the Bay of Selma, where the great fort of Dun Usneachain lay black against the ivy-clad heights beyond.

This was in the first heats of summer, and Nathos and Darthool, with Ailne and Ardan, had left the fort and were among the rocky declivities of the woodland near the sea. There they had three hunting booths: one for Nathos and Darthool, one for Ailne and Ardan, and one wherein to have their eating and drinking. In front of one of these booths

Nathos and Darthool sat, on that day of the days, playing on the *Cemrcaem* (the chess-board), the very chess-board which had belonged to Concobar, but which the king had left in the dun of Ailne and Ardan when hunting near by, on the day before that on which they fled with Nathos. It was all of ivory, and the chessmen were of wrought gold and in the likeness of strange kings and priests and fantastic animals wrought in immemorial years in the Orient.

And while they were playing a great shout was heard, coming upon them from a branch-hid hollow of the sea.

" That is the voice of a man of Erin," said Nathos, holding in the air a golden knight.

" Not so," answered Darthool ; " it is the voice of a Gael of Alba." Yet well she knew that Nathos had guessed aright, and that even now were the footsteps of fate drawing close. For none can prevail against destiny.

Once more a loud cry was heard, and a voice called upon Nathos and the sons of Usna.

" Of a surety, that is the voice of a man of Erin," said Nathos eagerly, for his heart was fain to see an Ultonian again, and to hear of the Red Branch and of the fate of

Uladh, and as to whether Concobar reigned still.

"Indeed, it is not so," answered Darthool, and turning the great glory and beauty of her eyes upon Nathos she bade him play on. Then a third cry, nearer and clearer, was heard ; and now all knew that it was the voice of a man of Erin.

"And if there be no cloud upon me," said Nathos, "that is the voice of no other than Fergus, the son of Rossa the Red, whom I knew well of old, and for whom my heart is fain.  Ardan, do ye go down at once to the haven, and bid Fergus welcome, and all who may be with him.  It is a good day this for us, when once more we may hear the voices of the Red Branch."

While Ardan went to the haven, Darthool told Nathos she had known from the first that the newcomer was a man out of Erin, and moreover, that he came from Concobar, and that his coming boded no good.

" And how will you be knowing the one and the other, Darthool ? "

" From a dream that I had : to wit, that three birds flew hither from Emain Macha, and brought with them three sips of rare honey, and then that they left us with that honey but took away instead three sips of our blood."

" Tell me, my queen, what is the reading you put upon that dream ? "

" That Fergus comes to us with the honey-words of peace, but that behind them lies the shedding of blood, and that blood ours."

Meanwhile Ardan welcomed Fergus, and brought him and his companions to where Nathos sat playing with Darthool upon the ivory and gold chessboard of Concobar the king. As the fair-smiling Ultonian drew near, he smiled a grimmer smile behind his beard, to see Nathos there with the two chiefest treasures of the king's heart—the woman he wished to make his queen, and the chessboard that had come to him from some great king's palace in the dim remote Indies of which the poets sang.

Great was the rejoicing, and Nathos and his brothers and Darthool embraced Fergus and his sons, and eagerly questioned them for tidings.

" The best tidings I have," Fergus answered, " is that I have come to ye with messages of loving peace from Concobar, whose heart is smitten by your long absence, and who would fain see in Erin again the three noblest lords in his or any other realm. Moreover, he has sent me to you with covenants and guarantees of loving good faith. He has pledged his kingly word, and I, too, have pledged mine, and ye know well, ye sons of Usna, that Fergus MacRossa Rua is not a man of light word. So come back to Erin with me, Nathos and Ailne and Ardan, and I pray of thee, come thou too, Darthool, wife of Nathos. Great shall be the welcome given to ye all, and sure it is a good thing to end a feud, and to put an unwaking sleep upon the sword and the spear."

"That is a good word," said Nathos, who was well pleased; but a sob was in the heart of Darthool, and her lips quivered as she spoke.

"Surely," she said, "Concobar MacNessa forgets. The sons of Usna are no tributaries. Nathos is overlord now of a country greater in extent than all the province of Uladh over which Concobar is king. It ill befits a king of an isle to go as a forgiven guest to the lord of a rock."

"That is true," said Fergus quickly, "Darthool has justice for what she says. But there is truth in what I say also, and it is a truth which the sons of Usna know, and will act by, that a man longs to see the land which is his own land or the land of his adoption. And were not Nathos and Ailne and Ardan among us as children and as boys and as youths, and are they not heroes of the Red Branch? Surely, it is a good thing for a man to see his own land each day, and to rejoice therein?"

"We have two lands," interrupted Ardan, "we who are of both Alba and Erin. Nevertheless, it would ill befit us not to look upon ourselves of the Red Branch first and foremost. So if Nathos is ready to go with thee, so also are Ailne and I myself."

"I am ready," said Nathos, though he kept his eyes away from those of Darthool.

"And ye know that my guaranty is sure?" added Fergus.

"It is sure," said Nathos.

That night all were full of joyous pleasure, save only Darthool, who in her heart knew that the shadowy feet of Fate were all about them, and that she at least and perhaps none other there would ever again see Alba.

On the morrow all set sail. As they left

the beautiful shores, than which for sure there
are none more beautiful in all the realms
of the Gael, Darthool took her harp and sat
back among the deerskins in the stern of the
galley and sang :

> "*Ionmhuin tir, an tir ud shoir—*
> *Alba go na h'-iongantaibh ;*
> *Nocha ttiocfainn aiste ale,*
> *Muna ttagainn le Naoise,*"

and for eight other verses in the old ancient
Gaelic that has lived in her lament till this
day : [1]

Dear is this land to me, dear is this land :
O Alba of the lochs !
Sure I would not be sailing sad from thy foam-white sand
Were I not sailing with Nathos for the Irish strand.

---

[1] This is a free paraphrase of the original as given by
Dr. Cameron in the *Reliquiæ Celticæ*.   The original con-
sists of nine short quatrains.   In the second, the names
mentioned are Dun Fiodha, Dun Fionn, Innis Droighin,
and Dun Suibhne.   In the following quatrains the old and
modern names are practically identical.   The modern
Glendaruel was formerly Glendaruay (Gleann da Ruadh),
the Glen of the Two Roes, or Glennaruay (Gleann na
Ruadh), the Glen of the Roes.   Innis Droighin is again
alluded to in the last verse.   It is now called Innis Draigh-
neach, meaning the Island of Thorns, and is situate in Loch
Awe.

# SONS OF USNA

Dear is the Forest Fort and high Dunfin,
And Dun Sween, and Innis Drayno—
Often with Nathos have I striven to win
To the wooded heights of these—and now we go
Far hence, and to me it is a parting of woe.


O woods of Coona, I can hear the singing
Of the west wind among the branches green
And the leaping and laughing of cool waters springing,
And my heart aches for all that has been,
For all that has been, my Home, all that has been !


Fain would I be once more in the woods of Glen Cain,
Fain would I sleep on the fern in that place :
Of the fish, venison, and white badger's flesh I am fain
That plentifully we had there, or wherever our trail
Carried us, yea, I am fain of that place.


Glenmassan ! O Glenmassan !
High the sorrel there, and the sweet fragrant grasses :
It would be well if I were listening now to where
In Glenmassan the sun shines and the cool west wind
        passes,
Glenmassan of the grasses !


Loch Etive, O fair Loch Etive, that was my first home,
I think of thee now when on the grey-green sea—
And beneath the mist in my eyes and the flying foam
I look back wearily,
I look back wearily to thee !


Glen Orchy, O Glen Orchy, fair sweet glen,
Was ever I more happy than in thy shade ?
Was not Nathos there the happiest of men ?

O may thy beauty never fade,
Most fair and sweet and beautiful glade.


Glen of the Roes, Glen of the Roes,
In thee I have dreamed to the full my happy dream :
O that where the shallow bickering Ruel flows,
I might hear again, o'er its flashing gleam,
The cuckoos calling by the murmuring stream.


Ah, well I remember the Isle of the Thorn
In dark and beautiful Loch Awe afar :
Ah, from these I am now like a flower uptorn,
Who shall soon be more lost than a falling star,
And am now as a blown flame in the front of war !


Nathos was sad when he heard this lament from the mouth of Darthool, and Ailne and Ardan looked at each other and whispered that it was the beginning of the end. Nevertheless, they did not fear to confront the days to come, for whatsoever the decrees of Fate may be a brave man does not draw back, but goes forward upon the way set before him. But Nathos was in a dream, and so heeded little, content too to chide Darthool because that she laid so much stress on vain imaginings.

The voyage was a swift and good one, and even Darthool's heart beat the quicker when once more she stood on the soil of Erin, her own land. In three days thereafter they came within sight of the Dun of Borrach, and Fergus MacRossa was glad, for soon he would be able to see Concobar the king, and tell him how great was his success.

It is a strange thing that a man such as Fergus Honeymouth could be so blind. Yet had he ever believed in the kinglihood of Concobar, and it was not till he reached the house of the son of Cainte that he knew in truth how the high king meant to play him false, and mayhap to deal treacherously with the sons of Usna. For after Borrach had greeted them all with affection and heartsome pleasure, he told them that word had come from Concobar that they were to press forward without delay, so great was the king's longing to see them again, and so deep was his love for three of the noblest of the knights of the Red Branch. "But upon thee, Fergus MacRossa, I have a feast made ready, a festival of weeks, and thou knowest it is *geas* upon thee not to refuse any feast made for thee: and so as thou wouldst avoid putting shame upon me and deep disgrace upon thyself, thou must abide here with me."

At that, Fergus flushed a deep red,[1] and was filled with anger. Yet could he not refuse, for his *geas* was sacred: and no man of that age dared break that bond.

So he turned to those with him, and asked what was now to be done.

"Let this be done," said Darthool: "either forsake the sons of Usna, or keep to thy feast-bond."

"My feast-bond I must keep, Darthool, yet will I not forsake the sons of Usna. My guaranty is known for sure: but over and above that I will send with them, and with thee, my two sons, Illann the Fair and Buine the Fiery, as further warranty."

But at these words Nathos turned away with a scornful smile.

"It is not at thee or thy feast-bond I smile, O Fergus," he said, "but at thy protection, good though thy sons be. For, by the Sun and Wind, I have never yet had need of any man to protect me, and go now, as ever before,

---

[1] Literally "O d'chuala Feargus sin, do rinneadh rothnuall corcra dhe O bhonn go bathas." (When Fergus heard this, he became a crimson mass from the foot-sole to the face.)

confident in my own valour and might: and this I say not boastingly, but openly, so that Concobar and all Uladh may know it."

Thereafter Darthool and the sons of Usna left the house of Borrach, and fared southward, with Illann the Fair and Buine in their company. As for Fergus, he cursed his bond, but nevertheless assured himself, for, as he said over and over, if the whole five provinces of Erin were assembled on one spot, they would not be able to break the solemn pledge of his guaranty.

But on the way Darthool urged advice upon Nathos and his brothers.

"Let us go," she said, "to the isle of Cullen, between Erin and Alba, and there await the day when Fergus will fulfil his bond. In that way he shall still keep the obligation of his *geas*, and yet we shall escape the evil that I know well awaiteth us."

"That we cannot do," answered the sons of Usna, "for we are in honour bound now to the king. Moreover, we have the guaranty of Fergus MacRossa."

"It was an ill day when we came here trusting to that word," Darthool replied: but said no more then.

At dusk they reached the White Cairn on Sliav-Fuad, and it was not till after they had left the watch-tower behind them that Nathos saw that Darthool was no longer of their company. So he retraced his way, and came upon her sleeping a deep sleep, though she awoke suddenly as he drew near.

"Is sleep so heavy upon thee, fair queen?" he asked, when he saw her startled eyes and pale face.

"I was weary, Nathos. Yet it is not weariness that has done this, but a dream. I dreamed a terrifying and dreadful thing. I saw thee and Ailne and Ardan and Illann the Fair, but on not one of these was the head remaining, but only on Buine the Fiery."

"And what will be the meaning of that, Darthool?"

"That Buine will leave ye ere death comes, and that a bloody death will be upon each. Nathos, I pray of thee that thou wilt go straightway to Dun Delgan, where the great and noble lord Cuchulain is, and abide with him for a while. There we shall be safe. Listen, I pray thee: I see thine own shadow creeping up thee, and a dark cloud overhead, and a cloud of clotted blood it is by the same token."

"Fair woman, there is some guile upon thy delicate thin lips. Why shouldst thou see evil everywhere? Be assured that neither I nor Ailne nor Ardan will turn aside from our quest of Concobar the king."

Darthool sighed, and remembered some old wisdom she had heard from Lavarcam: that if misfortune will not come to a man swiftly, he will seek it and take it by the great boar-fangs and compel it to come against him.

But on the morrow, as they came within sight of Emain Macha, once more she gave counsel.

"Ye know well, Nathos and Ailne and Ardan, that in Emain Macha are three fair great houses of the king: that in one he himself is, with the nobles of Uladh who are his own following, and that in another are the wayfarers of the Red Branch, and that in a third are the women. Now I warn ye of this thing: that if Concobar welcome us into his own house and among the nobles of Uladh, all will be well: but that if he send us to the house of the Red Branch, that will mean a disastrous end to thee and to me."

They said nothing to that, and when they came late into Emain Macha they knocked at the gates of Concobar's house.

The messengers told the king that the sons of Usna, and Darthool, and the two sons of Fergus MacRossa, were without: whereupon he asked of those about him in what state of provision and comfort was the house of the Red Branch, and on hearing that there was abundance of food and drink and comfort, he bade the messengers return and conduct the newcomers to that place.

When that message was given, Darthool again gave counsel: but Illann the Fair was wroth thereat, and the others yielded. As for Nathos, he said only:

"Great is thy love, Darthool, queen of women : but great also is thy fearfulness."

At that Darthool smiled gravely, but said no more. Only in her heart she remembered what Lavarcam, in bitter irony, had told her once, that when a man foresaw evil and forefended it he was wise and strong in his courage, but that if a woman did the same she was timorous and whim-borne.

In the house of the Red Branch the strangers were rendered all honour. Generous and pleasant foods and bitter cheering drinks were supplied to them, so that the whole company was joyful and merry, save the sons of Usna, and Darthool, who were weary with their journeying.[1]

Thus after they had eaten and drunken, Nathos and Darthool lay down upon high couches of white and dappled fawn-skins, and played upon the gold and ivory chessboard.

It was at this time that a secret messenger came from Concobar to tell him if Darthool were as beautiful as when she fled from Erin. This messenger was no other than Lavarcam. The woman embraced Darthool tenderly, and kissed the hands and brow of Nathos. Then, looking upon them through her tears, she said :

" Of a surety it is not well for ye twain to be playing thus upon the second dearest thing in all the world to Concobar, Darthool being

---

[1] This sentence is literal after the old Gaelic as translated by Dr. Cameron. Apropos of the mention of the chessboard in the next sentence (as once before), it may be added that the ancient Celtic kings and lords had a passion for chess.

the dearest, and ye having taken both from him, Nathos, and now ye twain being in his house and in his power. And this I tell you now, that I am sent hither by Concobar to see if Darthool has her form and beauty as it was of old. Thy beauty then was a flame before his eyes, Darthool, and now it will be as a torch at his heart."

Suddenly Darthool thrust the chessboard from her.

"I have the sight upon me," she said in a strange voice with a sob in it.

"And what is that sight, my queen?" asked Nathos.

"I see three torches quenched this night. And these three torches are the three Torches of Valour among the Gael, and their names are the names of the sons of Usna. And more bitter still is this sorrow, because that the Red Branch shall ultimately perish through it, and Uladh itself be overthrown, and blood fall this way and that as the whirled rains of winter."

Then taking the small harp by her side, she struck the strings and sang:

A bitter, bitter deed shall be done in Emain to-night,
And for ages men will speak of the fratricidal fight;

And because of the evil done, and the troth unsaid,
Emain of dust and ashes shall cover Emain the White.

Of a surety a bitter thing it is thus to be led
Into the Red Branch house, there to be rested and fed,
    And then to be feasted with blood and drunken with
        flame,
And left on the threshold of peace silent and cold and
    dead.

The three best, fairest, and noblest of any name,
Are they all to be slain because of a woman's fame?
    Alas! it were better far there were dust upon my head,
And that I, and I only, bore the heavy crown of shame.

At that Nathos was silent awhile. He knew now that Darthool was right. He looked at his brothers : Ailne frowned against the floor, Ardan stared at the door, with a proud and perilous smile. He looked at Illann the Fair and at Buine the Fiery : Buine drank heavily from a horn of ale, with sidelong eyes, Illann muttered between his set teeth.

"This only I will say, Darthool," Nathos uttered at last, "that it were better to die for thee, because of thy deathless beauty, than to live for aught else. As for what else may betide, what has to be will be."

"I will go now," said Lavarcam, "for Concobar awaits me. But, sons of Usna and sons of Fergus, see ye that the doors and windows be closed, and if Concobar come against ye treacherously may ye win victory, and that with life to ye all."

With that Lavarcam left. Swiftly she sought Concobar, and told the king that it was for joy she knew now that the three heroes, the sons of Usna, had come back to Erin to dwell in fellowship with the Ardree and the Red Branch, but that it was for sorrow she had to tell that Darthool the Beautiful was no longer fair and comely in form and face, but had lost her exceeding loveliness, and was now no more than any other woman.

At first Concobar laughed at that; then as his jealousy waned he thought with sorrow of the loss of so great beauty; and then again his spirit was perturbed. So he sent yet another messenger on the same errand.

This was a man named Treandhorn. Before Concobar sent him to the house of the Red Branch he said:

"Treandhorn, who was it that slew thy father and thy brother?"

"Thou knowest, O King, that it was Nathos, son of Usna, who slew them."

Concobar smiled. "Now," he said, "go and do my behest."

When Treandhorn reached the house, he found all the doors and windows closed and barred. Then fear seized him, for he knew that the sons of Usna were on guard, and would have wrath upon them.

Nevertheless, still more did he fear to go back to Concobar with nought to tell him.

So the man, descrying a narrow window at one side, climbed to it from an unyoked chariot that was near, and looked in. He saw Nathos and Darthool talking each to each in low voices, where they lay upon the white and dappled fawn-skins, with the gold and ivory chessboard between them. He smiled grimly, when he saw how great and noble and kingly Nathos seemed, and how more wonderful and beautiful than ever were the wonder and beauty of the eyes and face and form of Darthool.

It was the last time he smiled. At that moment Nathos glanced upward. Swift as thought he lifted a spiked and barbed chess-man and hurled it at the man's eye. Treandhorn fell backward, but rose at once and fled, with his right eye torn and blind for evermore.

When he came to the king and told his tale, and how Nathos was like a king indeed, and Darthool more beautiful by far than she had been of old, Concobar sprang to his feet. A red light came into his eyes, and he threw back his head and laughed ; and at that laughing every man there knew that his madness was come upon him, and that the blood-thirst was already sweating upon many swords.

"Ultonians," he cried, "will ye do the will of your king ? "

"That will we !" they answered with a great shout.

"Then come ye, and all your followers and vassals, and surround the house of the Red Branch, and set it in a forest of red flames, and if any run from out thereof put them to the sword."  As all ran swiftly from the king's fort, a high terrible voice was heard.  It was that of the dying Cathba the ancient Druid, and what he cried thrice was : "The Red Branch perisheth !  Uladh passeth !  Uladh passeth !"

But none heard him or paid heed, save only Lavarcam, who in that bitter crying knew well that the end was come.

In a brief while thrice three hundred men

surrounded the fort of the Red Branch, and set red flames about it; and thrice three hundred more made haste to join them.

There was a mighty onset at the first led by Buine the Fiery, who slew many, and quenched the fires, and threw the Ultonians into confusion.

"Who is the hero who has done this?" cried Concobar.

"It is I, Buine Borbruay, the son of Fergus MacRossa."

"I will give thee great bribes, Buine, if thou wilt forsake these robbers of my wife that was to be."

"What are thy bribes?"

"I will give thee a cantred of land at thine own choice, and I will make thee my chosen comrade, and thou shalt be as next to the king."

Then Buine the Faithless laughed and said: "Better the honours of a king than the thanks of dead men," and with that, for all the pledged guaranty of Fergus and the troth of his own word, he went over unto Concobar.

But when Illann the Fair heard of this he was wroth. He saw the bitter smile on the lips of Darthool, and he swore that he would not desert those upon whom lay the protection of his father's guaranty.

Meanwhile Ardan lay, dreaming with a proud smile against the fire ; and, upon the deerskins near the couch of Darthool, Ailne and Nathos played at chess, for little did they care to heed the treacherous valour of the Ultonians. They knew, too, that their hour was come ; and being kingly, gave no thought to that little thing.

But Illann called the troops together and fared forth, and made so deadly an onslaught that he slew three hundred of Concobar's men. Then he quenched the fires, and went back to the fort and to where Ailne and Ardan were playing together.

"Is that rain that is making a noise without ?" said Ailne to Nathos.

"No ; it is a humming of gnats," answered Nathos.   "Let us play on."

"My fate is heavy upon me, Nathos and Ailne," said Illann the Fair.   "I have done well by thee, but I feel the heavy hand of fate is against me, and who can withstand fate ?"

"No one," Nathos answered later, when he had thought upon his play.   At that Illann the

Fair drank a drink,[1] and went out again.   The
fires had been quenched, and there was a deep
darkness.   So he bade each man take a torch,
and then all set furiously again upon the Ultonians.

It was then that Concobar bethought him of
his son Fiacha the Fair, who was born on the
same night as Illann the Fair.   There was life
to the life, or death to the death, in that.

So he called Fiacha, and bade him strive
with Illann, and gave him the three famous
weapons of the royalty of Uladh—the moaning
Orchaoin, and the terrible Corrthach, and the
Notched-Bow.

But for all his enchanted weapons Fiacha
did not prevail, and after a great and wonderful
fight, which was girt about by a strange sighing,
the sighing being the breath of the pulses of the
watching host, Illann drove him to the ground
where he crouched behind the shelter of his
shield.   Easily then he might have slain him
but for this :—

The moaning Orchaoin made so great and
terrible a voice that it was heard afar off.
The Three Ceaseless Waves of Erin heard it,

[1] *Agus d'ibh deoch, agus tainigh amach aris*, etc., "and
he drank a drink," etc.

and roared responsive, so that all the coasts shook with their thunder: the Wave of Toth (*Tuaithe*), the Wave of Clidna (*Cliodhna*), and the Wave of Rudhraya (*Rudhraighe*). There was a great dun on these coasts, named Dun Tobairce, and there Conall Cernach the son of Amergin lived: and when he heard the roaring of the Three Waves of Erin, he knew that Concobar was in dire distress.

And that moaning of Orchaoin brought Conall Cernach on his magic steed that could fly through the night. He had with him his great sword "Blue Blade," and when he came to the place of the strife he moved swiftly up behind Illann the Fair, and plunged "Blue Blade" into the back, and through the heart, and out at the breast of the hero.

But when Conall Cernach heard from Illann's own lips what he had done, he was filled with wrath and grief.

"Thy faithless summons shall avail nought," he cried into the torchlit darkness where Concobar was; and with that he took his sword, and severed from its body the head of Fiacha the son of Concobar, and tossed it towards the king. Then, turning his back upon the host, he departed as he had come.

With the death of Illann the Fair, the Ultonians once more took heart. They surrounded the Red Branch fort, and again set red flames leaping against it.

Then Ardan came forth: laughing lightly, and with a proud joy.

The Ultonians saw then what it was to perish as mown grass. And when he had slain five times fifty, his arms grew weary.

"How many did Illann the Fair slay in that onslaught of his?" he asked.

"Thrice five score," he was told.

So Ardan slew two score and ten more, and then another score, for it did not befit so great a hero to slay less than an Ultonian champion, noble as Illann the Fair was.

When he was tired, he went into the fort, and told Ailne that there was still fresh carrion enough for a wild-hawk to glut its thirst with.

So Ailne rose from the chessboard and drank a drink, and went out, and did among the Ultonians even as Ardan had done, although he slew a score more, for he was older than Ardan, and so it did not befit him to put the stiffness and the silence upon fewer men.

Two-thirds of the night were now gone, yet Concobar did not withstay his wrath. For now the whole host of the Ultonians was gathered together, and he thought to have victory at the last.

But at their great shouting and the higher leaping of the flames Nathos rose. He kissed Darthool, then he drank a drink, and went out against the Ultonians.

In that hour thrice three hundred men grew cold and stiff.

Then he slew five score more.

"Go to Concobar," he said to a man, "and tell him that he has lost a thousand men over and above the hundreds slain by Illann the Fair and Ailne and Ardan. And now let him come to me himself."

But when Concobar heard that, he sent a messenger to Lavarcam to ask if Cathba the Druid were yet dead; and when he heard that he was not, he bade that the old man should be brought to him on a litter.

When Cathba was brought, he asked if the king meant death to the sons.

"I swear I mean no death," said Concobar; "but only honourably to subdue them and to obtain Darthool. And so I pray of thee to put an enchantment upon them, otherwise they will slay every Ultonian in the land."

So Cathba raised himself, and put an enchantment between the sons of Usna and the host of the Ultonians. That enchantment was a hedge of spears, taller than the tallest spear-reach, and more thickset than thorns on a bramble-bush.

But Nathos and Ailne and Ardan put their shields about Darthool, and came forth from the blazing house, and cleft a way through the hedge of spears, and, laughing loud, garnered a red harvest among the swaying corn of the Ultonian host.

Then there was a strange roaring heard, and a vast and terrible flood came pouring from the hills. The Ultonians fled to the high ground, but Darthool and the sons of Usna were cut off by the rushing waters.

Soon the flood rose to their waists, but then it ceased rising.

" The wind will soon blow," whispered Darthool, "and then the flood will rise, and we shall be drowned."

Nathos answered nothing, but raised her in his arms, and kissed her thrice upon the lips. Then he put her upon his left shoulder, where she sat with her white arms round his neck.

There was a smile in the blue eyes of Nathos.

The flood now subsided, but the sons of Usna could not move, for their feet were in a morass. On a dry spit of land close to them a man walked. This man was Maine of the Red Hand, a man of Lochlin,[1] in the train of Concobar.

Concobar had bidden some hero go forth and slay the sons of Usna. But none would stir. A deep shame burned in all. But Maine's father and two brothers had been slain by Nathos, and he said he would do likewise unto the sons of Usna.

When he drew near, Ardan spoke.

"Slay me first," he said, "for I am the youngest of the sons of Usna : and it may be that with my death the tides of fortune may flow again."

"That cannot be," said Nathos. "Here is the sword which Manannan, the son of Lir, gave me, and that cannot leave any remains of blow or stroke. Let this man Maine take it, and strike at us at one and the same time, so that not one of us may have the shame and sorrow of seeing the other beheaded."

[1] Scandinavia.

And so it was.  But while the man reached for the sword, Darthool sprang from the shoulder of Nathos, and strove to kill Maine of the Red Hand.  With a blow he reeled her aside, and then whirled the great sword of Manannan on high.

There was a flash in the air, and then the heads of the three fairest and noblest heroes of Alba fell.  There was a long and terrible silence, till suddenly the whole host of Uladh broke into lamentation.  Only Concobar stood leaning on his sword, and stared at the stillness that was now fallen upon the House of Usna.

But already afar off Darthool had descried the champion Cuchulain, and she fled towards him.

" Thou shalt be safe with me, beautiful one," he said.  " Tell me what thou wantest me to do."

" I do not wish to live, but I wish to live yet a brief hour, and not to be taken in shameful life before the eyes of Concobar."  So the twain returned to where the dead lay. Darthool fell upon her knees, and spread out the glory of her hair, and put her lips to the blood-wet lips of Nathos.

Then she rose, and looking upon the silent Ultonians, chanted this chant :


Is it honour that ye love, brave and chivalrous Ultonians ?
Or is the word of a base king better than noble truth ?
Of a surety ye must be glad, who have basely slain honour
In slaying the three noblest and best of your brotherhood.


Ardan the Proud, where now lies his yellow hair ?
Ailne the Comely, where now stare his sightless eyes ?
Nathos, the king of men, where now is his might, his
    glory ?
Where are the sons of Usna whom ye swore to honour ?


Let now my beauty that set all this warring aflame,
Let now my beauty be quenched as a torch that is spent—
For here shall I quench it, here, where my loved one lies,
A torch shall it be for him still through the darkness of
    death.


And with that Darthool stooped, and lifted the head of Nathos, and cleaned it of blood and foam, and the sweats of death, and kissed the eyes and the lips, and put her love upon the dear face, and her sorrow upon it, and her grief upon it, and put it to her white breast, and to her lips again, and gave it again her grief and her love.

Then at the bidding of Cuchulain three graves were digged. In each grave a son of

Usna was placed, and as each stood there his head was placed upon his shoulders.

But the grave of Nathos was made wider. Darthool stood therein and held his hands in hers, and put her lips often to his lips, and often whispered to him.

One other death there was in that hour, and in that place.

Cathba the Druid died there: and again he cried: "The Red Branch perisheth! Uladh passeth! Uladh passeth!"

And so it was. On the morrow Emain Macha fell before a great host, and was thenceforth a place of ruin and wind-eddied dust. The Red Branch became as scattered leaves, and were no more. And Uladh was given over to blood and rapine, and Concobar died in a madness of grief, and throughout Erin for many years the tides of death rose and fell.

But the sons of Usna slept, and the world dreams still of the beauty of Darthool.

# Notes

# Notes

## I

IN my renderings of the three famous ancient Gaelic
tales, collectively known as "The Three Sorrows of
Story-Telling" (*Tri Thruaighe na Scéalaigheachta*),
I have followed Professor Eugene O'Curry (*In Atlan-
tis, Manners and Customs*, and *MS. Materials*); Dr.
Douglas Hyde (*The Three Sorrows of Story-Telling*,
translated into English verse); Dr. Joyce (*Old Celtic
Romances*); Dr. Cameron (*Reliquiæ Celticæ*); Alex-
ander Carmichael (*Trs. Gael. Socy. of Inverness*); Dr.
Angus Smith (*Loch Etive and the Sons of Uisnach*).

These tales have often been retold in prose and
verse ; and particular intention should be made of
the metrical versions of Dr. Douglas Hyde, Dr.
Robert Joyce (*Deirdre*), and, I believe, of Dr. John
Todhunter.

In "The Children of Lir" I have closely followed
the version of the original, as translated by Dr. P. W.
Joyce (*Old Celtic Romances*), and in "The Sons of
Usna" the literal prose rendering by Dr. Cameron
and the metrical translation of Dr. Douglas Hyde.
These two stories are told more completely than that
of "The Sons of Turenn," which in the original ex-
tends to great length, as there the narrative of the
world-wide quest of the Sons of Turenn is given with
great detail.

Naturally in these retold ancient tales I have often followed the Scoto-Gaelic variants, both because of familiarity and by preference, and this particularly in the tale of "Darthool and the Sons of Usna."

Much the most ancient of the "Three Sorrows" is the tale of the Sons of Turenn. Professor O'Curry's version in *Atlantis* is the basis of all other modern renderings. The period of this tale belongs to mythological times. "The Children of Lir" may be taken as a connecting link between the mythological and prehistoric and Christian periods. The tale of "Deirdre," or "Darthool," is by far the best known in Gaelic Scotland, and is still the favourite ancient tale throughout all Gaeldom.

The reader who wishes further information should consult in particular Professor Eugene O'Curry; Dr. Cameron, in *Reliquiæ Celticæ*; Dr. Joyce, in *Old Celtic Romances*; and Dr. Douglas Hyde, in his delightful and deservedly popular little volume.

## II

The quatrains and other metrical pieces interpolated here, and those in the text of the first and third of these tales, are generally free renderings of the originals. Occasionally they are almost literal. But, both in the matter of selection and rejection, I have taken certain slight advisable liberties with the original versions. It may be as well to add, although already explained in the footnote at page 122, that the "Song to Macha" is here adapted from another poem known as "Crede's Lament" (*vide Silva Godelica*, Professor Sullivan's translation, etc.).

### III

" Darthool and the Sons of Usna." Readers familiar only with the Irish versions of this beautiful old tale should also consult the important variants given by Dr. Cameron and Mr. Alexander Carmichael. Dr. Angus Smith also gives a good digest, and readers interested in the Scottish wayfarings of Darthool and Nathos will find the details given there more or less specifically.

### IV

In the story of " The Sons of Turenn " it is possible that some injustice has been done to the character of Lugh, the foremost personage in it, best known in all the Gaelic chronicles as Lu-Lamfada—Lugh of the Long Hand. In this version he is represented uniformly as sternly cruel ; but it must be borne in mind that his inveterate hostility to the Sons of Turenn was not due to insatiable revenge alone, but to his belief (as prophesied by his father) that any clemency in the fulfilment of the great eric demanded would result in terrible disaster to Erin itself. Throughout this ancient tale, indeed, we recognise Lu-Lamfada as an impersonation of Destiny or Nemesis. It may at the same time be added that in the story of " Darthool " Fergus is shown more obviously culpable than the old chronicles indicate, where he appears rather as a too innocent and trustful tool of King Concobar.

### V

A few notes as to the less familiar of the Gaelic names introduced in the foregoing pages may aptly be given here, and the more conveniently in alphabetical order.

AÉ. Pronounced as rhyming to day: equivalent to Hugh.

AILNE. The older forms are *Ailna* and *Ainlé*. The latter (pronounced Anlă) is probably the right name. It is said to signify beauty.

ALBA. The Gaelic for Scotland. The genitive of this word is Alban, whence the familiar English word for Scotland, Albyn.

BANBA. This was one of the three ancient names of Ireland—Banba, Fola, and Eiré—the names of three famous queens of antiquity. It is from the last that Ireland derives its best known Gaelic name.

BOVE DERG (*Bodbh Dearg*). This semi-mythical king was one of the old Dedannan race, and stands, as it were, midway between the elder gods and the historic heroes. His name in Ireland is commonly pronounced Bove-d'Yarrag; and in Scotland as Bove Derg.

CONOR (*Connachar*). The oldest form of this famous Gaelic name, so common in Ireland, is Concubair, or Concobar. Dr. Hyde says that Concubair is properly pronounced Cunnhoor, but doubtless Concobar is closer to the ancient usage.

CUCHULAIN. The oldest form of the name of this great Gaelic hero is Cuchulaind. The name is pronounced Coo-hoolin, whether spelled according to any of the Irish-Gaelic variants or as to the Scottish Cuthullin—but sometimes, as in Skye, Coolin. It is not the real name of the hero in question. The word signifies the hound of Culainn, and innumerable references to Cuchulain are found throughout early Irish literature simply as The Hound. He was a native prince of Ulster, and lord of the district of Muirthemne, lying between and including the present towns of Dundalk and Drogheda, now called the County of Louth, where his chief residence was named Dun Delga (Dundalk). This celebrated hero, the champion of the knights of the great order of Gaelic chivalry, known as the Red Branch, was the son of Soalte, or Sualtam, and of Decteré, sister of the celebrated Irish king, Concobar mac Nessa (a contemporary of Christ). His name was Setanta, but he was commonly known as Cu-Culainn, the Hound of Culaan, who was his instructor and war-smith to King Concobar. The most famous of the Knights of the Red Branch at this time were the heroes known as Fergus mac Róigh, Conall Cearnach, Fergus mac Leité, Curoi mac Dairé, and Cuchulain mac Soalte.

DAGDA, or THE DAGDA. This is a purely mythical personage, and is one of the ancient Gaelic divinities, among whom he occupies a place somewhat akin to that of Jupiter in the Latin Pantheon.

DEDANNAN. Pronounced Day-Donnan. This is the colloquial form of the Tuatha-De-Danann ; that is, the elder semi-divine inhabitants of Ireland, mostly mythical, and in some cases euhemerised. They became the Hidden People, or People of the Hills, of ancient Gaelic legend, and later the Fairies of popular tradition, though now the drift of poetic thought is towards a restoration of the Tuatha-De-Danann to their old spiritual significance and empery. The term signifies the Divine Progeny of Ana, a mysterious and perhaps supreme ancient goddess.

The Dedannans were also called The Deena-Shee (Daoine-Sidhe), or Fairy Folk; the Aes-She, or People of the Hills; the Marcra-Shee, or Fairy Cavalcade; and the Sloo-She (Sluagh-Sidhe), or Fairy Host.

DUN. This word is properly pronounced Doon, though in Gaelic Scotland generally Dun. It signifies a fortress or great fortified dwelling or encampment, and should not be confused with Rath, which is more what we would call the homestead, hamlet, village, or township, according to circumstances; or, with Lis, or Lios, a smaller fort probably corresponding to what we call a keep.

EILIDH. The name Eilidh is pronounced Eily (*Isle-ih*), and is said to be the Gaelic equivalent of Helen.

EMANIA. This is simply the Latinized form of *Emhain*, or *Emain*, the capital of North Ireland in the ancient days. The name is variously pronounced as Emain, Avvin, and Yew-an or Yow-an.

ERIC. Originally eiric, pronounced ay-ric. Signifies literally a fine or blood-money, and is perhaps best rendered in English by the word ransom.

FELIM. This name is more familiar as Phelim. The modern Gaelic is Phelimy, and the older, Pedlimid.

GEASA. Pronounced Gassa. It is the plural of *geis* (often written *geas*), and signifies oath-bound injunctions or undertakings. In the old days for a man to be under *geasa* meant that he was solemnly bound to do such and such a thing, or, as it might be, to refrain; and the bond once taken could not be broken without loss of honour.

# NOTES

ILDANNA.   The old Irish word is best represented by Il-danach, that is, the Master of Craft, or Master of the Many Arts, and is a name which is specifically given to Lugh Lamfada, Lugh the Long-Handed.

ILLANN.   This frequent name of Illann, or Illan, is identical with Ullin, so familiar in Scotland through the famous poem of " Lord Ullin's Daughter."

LIR.   Pronounced sometimes Lirr, but generally Lear.

LOCHLANN.   A general name for the whole of Scandinavia, including, of course, Denmark, and not, as sometimes stated, of Norway only.

LUGH.   This name is pronounced Lu, or Loo, and I have so given it in the text.

MANANNAN.   Pronounced Mon-on-awn.   He is the Neptune of Gaelic mythology, but holds a more mysterious and more potent position in the Gaelic Pantheon than his classical congener.

MAEV.   The name of this most famous queen of antiquity is variously spelt.   The original is Meadb, or Medbh, and is properly pronounced Mave (rhyming with wave).

MURHEMNE.   The original of this is Magh Muir-teimne, pronounced Moy-mwir-hev-na.   It is the plain from the Boyne to near Carlingford.

MOYLE.   This is the commonest pronunciation of the old Gaelic Maol, though the word is best known in Scotland as Mull (from the Mull of Cantyre).   It is applied to the sea between Cantyre and Ulster.

MEKWEEN.   The original of this difficult name is Miodcaoin.   I do not know what it means.

NATHOS.   Originally Naisi ; later Naoise ; and commonly pronounced Neeshă.

NUADH. Pronounced Noo-ă.

OGAM, or OGHAM. The ancient Cryptic method of writing, like the Northern Runes, chiefly graven on funeral stones or monuments. The word is sometimes pronounced *Oo-am*, or *oom*, but Ogam is probably right according to ancient usage.

SHEE FINNAHA. The old Gaelic is Fhionncaid, and is properly pronounced Sheeh-Innăchee.

TAILKENN, or TAILCINN. This name for St. Patrick signifies Adze-Head (probably from his monkish tonsure).

TURENN. The old form is Tuireann, and is pronounced Tirran or Toorenn.

ULAD, or ULADH. The old name of Ulster, of which Ultonia is the Latinized form. Ulad is properly pronounced Ulla.

UR. This name is pronounced *oo-ar* (Gaelic, Uar). The name in its old form is Iuchar, as that of his brother is Iucharba, which I have given as Urba. It is probable, however, that Ur is the modern equivalent of Iucharba, and Yukar, or Yooch-ar (which I have given as Urba), of the third of the Sons of Turenn. There is great confusion and diversity in these old names.

By FIONA MACLEOD

# Green Fire

*Crown 8vo. 6s.*

"A brilliant romance of Celtic life, partly in an old chateau in Brittany, partly in an island in the Hebrides." — *St. James' Gazette.*

"Besides William Morris, now gone, there are few in whose hands the pure threads have been so skilfully and delicately woven as they have in Fiona Macleod's."—*Pall Mall Gazette.*

"The fuller revelation that was looked for from Miss Macleod's earlier works has been amply fulfilled in this volume."—*Western Mail.*

"The descriptive passages vibrate with colour and sound, at once delicate and vivid."—*Daily News.*

"Fiona Macleod carries us away at once from the modern realism into the realms of romance and mysticism. She is essentially the bard of the Celt."—*The Gentlewoman.*

"This clever exponent of Celtic legend and story is at her best in 'Green Fire.'"—*Literary World.*

"Once again has this clever author enchanted us."—*Publishers' Circular.*

"A gifted writer of Celtic romance."—*Morning Post.*

"The two scenes we have noted prove her to be a writer of rare ability."—*New Saturday Review.*

"The style of this book is sustained throughout at a very high level."—*Daily Telegraph.*

"She stands quite alone in her particular realm of fancy, and hardly less so in her method of giving it words."—*Saturday Review.*

"Full of poetry, passion, and beautiful descriptions."—*The Guardian.*

"The book possesses a weird fascination of its own: its pages are illuminated ever and anon by brilliant flashes of genius."—*The Lady.*

"Miss Macleod has rarely poured herself out more fully in profuse strains of rhythmic prose than in this Celtic tale."—*Athenæum.*

ARCHIBALD CONSTABLE & CO
2, WHITEHALL GARDENS, WESTMINSTER, S.W

# Songs for Little People

By NORMAN GALE

Profusely Illustrated by HELEN STRATTON

*Large Crown 8vo, 6s.*

"A delightful book."—*Scotsman.*
"We cannot imagine anything more appropriate as a gift-book for children."—*Glasgow Daily Mail.*
"This book, in truth, is one of the most tasteful things of its kind."—*Whitehall Review.*
"Mr. Norman Gale is to be congratulated."—*Black and White.*
"A delightful book in every way."—*Academy.*

# Tales from Hans Anderson

With Forty Illustrations by HELEN STRATTON

*Imperial 16mo, 2s. 6d. ; gilt extra, 3s. 6d.*

"Very acceptable to all young people."—*Gentlewoman.*
"We congratulate Miss Stratton. . . . Excellent work."—*Pall Mall Gazette.*

# The Kitchen Maid

OR

# Someone we know very well

A Play for children in Two Acts.

By MARY F. GUILLEMARD

With Illustrations by BERNARD PARTRIDGE, E. M. HALE, MARGERY MAY and HELEN STRATTON

*Foolscap Quarto, 3s. 6d.*

"The old story presented with a freshness which gives it a new charm altogether."—*Pall Mall Gazette.*
"With a proper regard for the tastes and intelligences of children."—*The Scotsman.*
"Very effectively illustrated by Bernard Partridge and others."—*The Record.*

## CONSTABLE'S LIBRARY OF

# Historical Novels and Romances

EDITED BY G. LAURENCE GOMME

*Crown 8vo, 3s. 6d., cloth extra.*

After a Design by A. A. TURBAYNE.

With Illustrations of all the principal features, which include reproductions of royal and historical signatures, coins, seals, and heraldic devices.

The first three volumes are :—

HAROLD : Lord Lytton's *Harold, the Last of the Saxons*, 1848.
WILLIAM I : Macfarlane's *Camp of Refuge*, 1844.
WILLIAM II : *Rufus or the Red King*, 1838 (Anonymous).

# The King's Story Book

Edited by G. LAURENCE GOMME.  With numerous full-page Illustrations by C. HARRISON MILLAR.  *Crown 8vo, cloth gilt, 6s.*

# A Houseful of Rebels

### A Fairy Tale.

By WALTER H. E. RHODES.  Illustrated by PATTEN WILSON.  *Crown 8vo, cloth gilt, 6s.*

# Beyond the Border

### Fairy Tales for Old and Young.

By WALTER DOUGLAS CAMPBELL.  With nearly 200 Illustrations by HELEN STRATTON.  *Crown 8vo, cloth gilt, 6s.*

# Adventures in Legend

### Tales of the West Highlands.

By the MARQUIS OF LORNE, K.T., M.P.

# Westward Ho!

By CHARLES KINGSLEY.  (Vol. 3 of Constable's Historical Novels.)  Edited by G. LAURENCE GOMME.

*Illustrated, crown 8vo, cloth gilt, 3s. 6d., and handsomely bound with cover design in gold, all gilt, 5s.*

# London Impressions

A Series of Pictures in Photogravure by WILLIAM HYDE, and Essays by ALICE MEYNELL.

Imperial Quarto, strictly limited to 250 signed copies. For particulars see Prospectus.

# Through China with a Camera

### By JOHN THOMSON, F.R.G.S.

With about 100 Illustrations.  Foolscap 4to.  This work contains the finest series of pictures of China ever published.

# By the Roaring Reuss

### Tales of a Simple Folk.

By W. BRIDGES BIRTT.  With Illustrations.  *Crown 8vo, cloth gilt, 6s.*

# The Dark Way of Love

By CHARLES LE GOFFIC
Translated by EDITH WINGATE RINDER.

# Medals and Decorations of the British Army and Navy

By JOHN HORSLEY MAYO.  Profusely Illustrated with Coloured and other Plates.  *2 vols., Royal 8vo, cloth gilt,* £3 3*s. net.*

# The Paston Letters

Edited by JAS. GAIRDNER.  A New Issue in three styles.  *3 vols., Foolscap 8vo.  Paper label and cloth,* 16*s. net ; Cloth gilt,* 16*s. net ; Half-vellum,* 21*s. net*

# The Principles of Local Government

By G. LAURENCE GOMME.  *Demy 8vo, cloth gilt.*

# The Pupils of Peter the Great

By J. NISBET BAIN.  With Portraits.
*Demy 8vo, cloth gilt.*

# Fidelis and other Poems

By C. M. GEMMER.
*Foolscap 8vo, cloth gilt.*

# A Tale of Boccaccio and Other Poems

By ARTHUR COLES ARMSTRONG.
*Crown 8vo, cloth gilt,* 5*s. net.*

# Songs of Love and Empire

By E. NESBIT.
*Crown 8vo, cloth gilt.*